Kári Gíslason  2.
He moved to d
then to Austral ...ast book,
The Promise of Iceland (UQP, 2011), told the story of return journeys that he has made to his birthplace, and in 2012 was shortlisted in the Queensland Literary Awards. Kári was awarded a doctorate in 2003 for his thesis on medieval Icelandic literature. As well as memoir and fiction, he publishes scholarly articles, travel writing and reviews. He currently lectures in Creative Writing and Literary Studies at Queensland University of Technology.

Bookclub notes for *The Ash Burner* are available at www.uqp.com.au.

PRAISE FOR *THE PROMISE OF ICELAND*

'A deeply charming account of displacement, of not really knowing where you come from and how that makes it difficult to know where you belong.' *The Sunday Mail* (Book of the Week)

'Landscape plays a large role in this gorgeously told tale; the extremes of the Australian landscape and the Icelandic one frame a tale of fathers, sons, mothers, betrayals, forgiveness and love. This is a quietly moving and affecting memoir.' Krissy Kneen, *Avid Reader*

'[A] memorable, finely-crafted book.' *The Age* (Non-Fiction Pick of the Week)

'This is one of the better kinds of memoir – one in which the author is not only reflective, but also reflexive. Kári demonstrates an awareness of the fallibility of memory, of subjectivity, and his own shortcomings as a writer and son.' Hannah Kent, *Readings Monthly*

'Gíslason makes a bittersweet journey home, where he receives an unexpected welcome.' *The Sun-Herald*

'A powerful memoir about landscape and identity.' *The Advertiser*

'What Gíslason does particularly well is make a case for the significance of place in people's lives ... The journeys to Iceland, then, a country beautifully realised in the book's pages, are truly stations on the author's bumpy, if often amusing, road to healing and self-knowledge.' *The Canberra Times*

'An honest, contemplative and heartfelt journey across generations, landscapes and ... the truth and mythology of family.' *Weekend Gold Coast Bulletin*

'With elegance and tenderness, Kári discusses the loves that have defined his life. Wise and unassuming, humorous and remarkably affecting all at the same time, *The Promise of Iceland* is an enchanting reflection of a fascinating life and a profound exploration of the human condition.' *Stilts*

The Ash Burner

KÁRI GÍSLASON

UQP

First published 2015 by University of Queensland Press
PO Box 6042, St Lucia, Queensland 4067 Australia

uqp.com.au
uqp@uqp.uq.edu.au

Cover design by Sandy Cull, gogoGingko
Author photograph by Nicholas Martin
Typeset in 12/17 pt Adobe Garamond by Post Pre-press Group, Brisbane
Printed in Australia by McPherson's Printing Group

Epigraph and quote on p. 200 from *Markings* by Dag Hammarskjöld, translated into English by
Leif Sjöberg and WH Auden, and published by Faber & Faber, London, 1964.

All attempts have been made to contact copyright licensees for permission to reproduce material.
If you believe material for which you hold rights is reprinted here, please contact the publisher.

Australian Government

This project has been assisted by the Australian Government
through the Australia Council, its arts funding and advisory body.

National Library of Australia
Cataloguing-in-Publication data is available at http://catalogue.nla.gov.au

ISBN 978 0 7022 53423 (pbk)
ISBN 978 0 7022 54765 (PDF)
ISBN 978 0 7022 54772 (epub)
ISBN 978 0 7022 54789 (Kindle)

University of Queensland Press uses papers that are natural, renewable and recyclable
products made from wood grown in sustainable forests. The logging and manufacturing
processes conform to the environmental regulations of the country of origin.

For friends lost and found

'So rests the sky against the earth'
– Dag Hammarskjöld

A dozen paces from the house, and I was onto the dune again. The day hot, but the depth of it locked under the road; the sand powdery as I ran beneath the low branches to the top. Tipped over it. Evenings on the path produced such quiet light. But as I came down, the dune dipped and caved into my own broken steps, towards the waves still afternoon blue, holding to that perfect invitation – the one that, in my mind, I held through slow days of lessons and wooden seats: to dive in and be back. To swim.

I try to recall the perfect confidence with which I did it, how easily it came. Ran in, and felt the grass and seeds and dust wash off. Up close, the water was suddenly dark. My feet disappeared in the shadow of a cloud, the deepening sea floor giving way. The entire world lay in the deep, I was sure of that. A child's philosophy, but more true as well, more certain. I knew that the world was connected along the ocean floor, and that its bass notes, my mother's heart, could only be heard there.

Now, I am no longer as sure. But my body still remembers the water as it reached around my waist and left its slip of thin waves. It feels the tide, and how it was stronger that day. How the threat was there, as I stepped in, and it pulled in irregular clutches at my legs, across the open beach. How I shouldn't have gone in.

But I did. I dived in. The best moment of any day, met in that overlay of sky and sea, when those two halves of the world are no longer separate but folded over and confused. Then you come up, take your first strokes, and the divide is formed again: sea and sky reconstructed along the silver road of the horizon. At the end of it lay my goal: a cliff, our fort at the southern tip of the beach. Lion's Head, a wounded outcrop of rocks and broken trees shaped as its name, a stately lion with its paws dipped into the sea.

I swam a long way out. Only when I reached the outer edge of what I could manage – the point at which I might not make it – would I begin to work my way to shore, in my mind following a wide curve back in. Sometimes, as a game that I played against my own fears, and perhaps against my hopes for adventure and the world down there, I imagined that I was being chased by something sinister, a monster or a shark. Once, it came true: a fin and sudden, hot fear.

Yet even then, as the grey passed me, the water contained only the feeling of home, for it was such an impossible luxury to swim, and such liberation from the heat of the summer: sweat under the knees, cut grooves in the sticky surface of the desk. In the water, I felt I'd accepted the invitation at last. I was back.

And as I swam, I reached down to find the ghost that every afternoon drew me into the water. I searched for my mother, certain that she remained with us here, if not in the everyday world. I looked for the rocks – a line of them that ran out from the Head. I pushed past to them, and waited for her to come. My legs lifted up towards the surface, as I hovered over the bottom for as long as I could hold my breath. Then, when I touched the seabed I heard again that bass note that connected and pulsed the world over. The ocean floor of us all. And somewhere along it, the voice of the dead.

The further out I went, the closer we became, and the more insistent the hidden theme. In this way, over time I had extended the swim until that Friday afternoon I must have been nearly a kilometre out; further than I could manage. The excitement of it: not only didn't I have control anymore, but I'd surrendered it to her. So when I saw the rip, the normal signs – a slick channel of water that tailed across the surface – I knew what it meant, but I didn't try to move out of its way. The current followed me, and soon enough my course had bent to it. I was pulled past the lion and towards its pride of breakers on the other side.

I wasn't frightened. Or, rather, I wasn't frightened enough. I knew that the sea had me; it was deciding where I was going next. Already, it was shaping a new life, even while I had the energy and maybe the chance to get out. But once I'd passed the Head I stopped resisting altogether. Let the tide take me somewhere. It seemed so obvious that there was some point to it. Isn't that what it means to be a child: that there can only ever be meaning?

So I stood treading water, and waited for the meaning to make itself known. My mother would come, I was sure she would come. And then together we'd know what was next.

But as I waited, I felt a shift, a change in perception away from the water under me. Something drew my eyes towards a figure on the uneven steps that led to the top of Lion's Head. He was running down from the lookout. And seeing him there, seemingly coming to help me, I realised that the true menace lay not in the waves or in the current, but in a first, light temptation to stop treading water.

Close your eyes, it said. And for a moment I did. I let the waves around me block the sight of the person on the lookout, and I let my head dip under the surface, into the warm salt water. Below, there was no current at all, no movement, all stillness and peace. I had escaped the rip, if I wished it. I could stay there, with her.

What was it, then?

A shot?

Yes, a shot fired from the rocks, Dad's voice – the man who'd run desperately down from the top of the Head to reach me. Along the surface, on the rocks, the sure sight of my father. And a horrible awareness of what he'd find if I let go. He yelled and I heard him more clearly. 'Come back!'

He dived in. I panicked, finally. But already the last strength out of me. I lost my breath, shaking. The water was cold. A hollow, deathly hunger. I began to cry. I called out for help, searched for him in the water. Where had he gone? Where was he? I wanted to stop.

But I couldn't see him.

1

Come back. He held my hand and pressed the words into my palm. 'Listen to me.' I heard his voice as though it were coming up through the pillow rather than from the faint presence next to me. But he spoke so little. What did he want me to hear?

I slipped in and out of a fever. I liked it, this other ocean of warmth and cold that seemed to be carrying me away. But then in stark moments it brought me back, with a heavy chest and a stomach that ached, a longing for something that hadn't been met but rather interrupted. I'd been saved.

'You're nearly there,' Dad said, but in the haze I couldn't decide whether he meant the rocks of Lion's Head or the room we were in, with the shadows that broke over it, too. Unsure, I thought to myself over and over: *He must have made it.*

He must have made it. It was Dad. But I was bleeding, a deep cut in my side made by the rocks as I finally reached them. He pulled me free. Blood collected in a shallow rock pool. That was a memory. And I remembered blood on Dad's wide hands as he lifted me. A hand against the side of my face as he held me.

And then, later, a hand on my temple, while I came out of the fever.

I slept and slept, and when at last I woke properly my eyes followed the changing light on the wooden frame of the window beside my bed. I wondered to myself if that was where God was – not on the ocean floor that connected the world, with all the answers it was meant to contain about my mother, but in the wooden cracks at the edge of the glass. In the splinters.

They kept the bed next to mine empty. It was perfectly quiet, so quiet that sometimes I thought I could hear my muscles twitching, and a thin percussion in my fingers when I lay on my hands. Eventually I made out the muffled sound of other children in a distant room somewhere – and a pounding that came through the floor, their steps on the floorboards, like nights when the surf was heavy and the drumming made it up to the house.

I sensed Dad was always there, although often I felt rather than saw his outline in the room.

And then one morning I woke up hungry.

He asked whether there was anything I wanted to eat. I told him I wanted something salty, and so my first meal when I came out of the worst days was a packet of crisps. Each morning, I still woke up panicking, still thinking I might drown. But gradually the room formed as a more definite reality, one that could replace those last minutes in the sea, and I saw instead the wooden panels, and pale curtains that let in the light.

Corner shadows concealed a single chair and a sliding table. A few of Dad's books were there: he was reading *The Quiet American* by Graham Greene, and the slim volume sat on top of the pile. When he came back into the room, he picked it up and sat with his side to me.

I pretended not to be awake; for a few minutes, the trick worked and we were back in his office and it felt like I was watching him read, waiting for him to light a cigar and sip his tea with scotch. But then he turned to me and put down the book, and through half-closed eyes I watched him struggle with what to say next.

He didn't once ask why I'd gone out so far on my own, but with that kindness to me he also spared himself a task that we should have undertaken then, while it was still fresh. We should have thought of ways of finding Mum together, not on our own as we'd done until now. But neither of us wanted to talk about it, not the accident nor what lay behind it.

For the outcome had been a kind of betrayal – a loss of faith in the solidarity of us – and that had to be said first if we were going to go any further. So instead he smiled at me and returned to his book, and I continued to watch him read.

After a week in this room, the muffled sounds next door found shape as laughter and yelling – and I was to be moved in to join them. *The Quiet American* and the pile beneath it were finished, and my father said he was going back to work.

'Who's been fighting?' I asked him. 'Any good cases lately?'

'Oh, just the usual suspects. Murphy wants his fences fixed again. The supermarket isn't paying its bills. But I've been asked to go to Sydney, Ted. I'm going to help with the drafting of a report. An old friend of mine teaches at the law school. He's asked me to help him.'

'I'll be alright,' I said.

'Listen, they want you in here for another couple of weeks. So I'll be back before you're out. Is there anything you'd like from Sydney?'

It felt like my only chance. 'Dad, I'm sorry.'

'I know you are. But is there anything I can get you?'

'I wish I hadn't done it.'

'I know. We'll be alright.' He stood up and got ready to leave, collected his portable library into his leather briefcase. He said he'd buy me something for my thirteenth birthday. Something to read while I was getting better.

'I won't swim again,' I promised.

'I know.' He pressed my hand.

I watched him leave, and when he didn't turn around to say goodbye I saw the anger he held in.

I felt it might help to have someone apart from him to talk to – to tell somebody else everything that I'd found out for myself, the things he hadn't explained to me. Someone to tell that my mother had drowned, and that that was why my father was so angry.

He passed into the corridor, and gradually the light movement of nurses and trolleys replaced his absence. I watched them as they rushed here and there, their familiar busyness like a curtain that swung open and closed across the doorway.

When the nurses spoke to me, there was a pleasing note of sexual teasing in their voices. They quizzed me about whether I had a girl-friend. I knew, in a way, that they were asking about Dad, not me, but I didn't mind that. They were curious, and I was an easy way to place the question.

'Of course I don't have a girlfriend,' I replied.

'That's a shame,' said one. 'You know that girls love a patient. You're almost ideal boyfriend material at the moment.'

'I doubt that.' But it was a thought, all the same.

In the new room, it was Anthony who started our first conversation. I'd seen him around town, and I had some idea of who he was. But I wouldn't have thought to speak to someone in the grade above me, in the high school I was about to join. And he was nearly two years older than me, one of the older ones in his year. Even now, I can see him sitting down on the end of my bed, uninvited.

'Are you going to show me?' he asked.

I'd noticed already that there was a fair bit of wound-swapping, so the request seemed natural enough. I lifted my shirt, and for a moment we joined in an inspection of the broad, white bandage that circled my torso. A spot of blood showed where the cut was deepest. The nurses had told me not to run around too much, for the wound kept bleeding lightly. I did as I was told, but they didn't believe me. To Anthony, I said that if you stared at it too long, the blood appeared to be moving towards the edges of the bandage, like a drop of red ink on blotting paper.

Anthony nodded. For a moment, I thought we were done. He stood up to go. He was tall and very lean. His hair was cropped short, and this made his dark eyes seem unnaturally large, as if held wide open. He was handsome. To me, he seemed completely out of place here. A visitor.

He still looked like he would leave, but then sat back on the end of my bed and said, 'Did you know that you nearly died?'

'No.'

'They couldn't treat your infection.'

'How do you know?'

He shook his head. It said, *We all know*. And then, 'Give me a second.' He walked across the room to his bed at the far end, near the windows, and when he came back he handed me a book. 'Have you read this?' It was an anthology of poems by Emily Dickinson.

9

'No.'

'Do you want me to leave it for you?' he said.

'No, thank you.'

'Don't you read poetry?'

'Not really. Sometimes Dad reads poems out loud. He likes WH Auden and Philip Larkin.'

'Well, I can't keep it. My dad wouldn't ...'

When Anthony didn't finish the thought, I asked, 'How did you get the book, then?'

'My girlfriend brought it for me. Claire. Do you know her?'

'I've seen her around,' I answered. 'I think I've seen her with you.'

Again, there was a pause during which Anthony might leave, and if he had, perhaps our friendship would have amounted to no more than this.

But I didn't want him to go yet. And what else do you ask someone in a hospital but their reason for being there?

'Can I see?'

So it was Anthony's turn to lift his shirt. He sat down, turned his back to me, and heard me catch my breath. He quickly pulled his shirt down again and faced me. His face was flushed.

'Is it that bad?'

'Yes,' I said. 'I mean ...' The bruise was all the way down his back.

He turned towards the door, watched the nurses coming and going. 'I'm fine now. I think they only keep me here because they know I don't mind it.' He added, 'Don't say anything. I haven't shown anyone before.'

'But how did it happen?'

'I'll tell you later. So, do you want the book?' he asked again.

'No.'

He stood up and put it down by my side. 'Give it to your dad, then.'

Anthony left me alone for the rest of the day. But after that, he was the most regular caller at my bedside. I didn't understand him very well. At first I didn't even know why he confused me, but gradually I realised that he had a way of speaking in ideas rather than events, in a way opposite to how my father spoke and what I was used to.

Like Dad, however, Anthony wore his curiosity very openly. He said that, after the Dickinson, he now *needed* to read more American poetry. Not even Dad had ever spoken about 'needing' writers. Anthony said he'd ask Claire for Whitman, but also more American women writers: Chopin, Jewett, Willa Cather.

I was curious about Claire, and how she dealt with these strange requests. 'How do you manage to read so much?' I asked.

His reply was, 'How can you lie there just thinking all that time?'

I wasn't sure. I didn't think about anything in particular, but it seemed that I needed the time not to. But to my surprise, I soon found myself waiting for him, hoping he'd make it across the room to share one of his thoughts or arguments.

His favourite topic was beauty. He said he *believed in it*.

'What is it, then?' I asked him. 'I don't think I get the point of beauty. Dad once said that Mum was almost *too* beautiful. Have you ever heard that before?'

No, but he liked the idea: 'That's exactly what I think, too. Beauty is when you feel overwhelmed, as though the person has done something to you.'

'The person?'

'The girl,' he replied, and smiled. 'Or, the world. Suddenly the world does something so lovely that it hurts. You must get that?'

I told him I liked the feeling of water running through my fingers, when I swam and stretched my arms forward. 'That's such a good feeling. I guess that's a beautiful feeling.'

'That's the feeling of being comfortable,' Anthony said. 'It's not the same.'

'Isn't that just as good?' I asked.

'No,' he replied. 'It has to hurt.'

Eric, our neighbour from next door, came most days and filled me in on my father's trip to Sydney. Dad would call him to check on the garden and the house, and to give him messages to pass on to me. Eric said that everything at the law school was on schedule, and Dad would be back well before it was time for me to come home.

This should have cheered me up, but it didn't quite work. I noticed that I wasn't in any rush to leave, and also that I was waiting to meet Anthony's girlfriend, Claire. After a few days in the main ward, her visits still hadn't coincided with when I was awake.

But I had visits from my class, and from my teacher Miss Weston who, despite having supposedly given up on an interest in my father, made it from the library to bring me books to read, along with my homework and goodwill messages from school. Other neighbours found me reading Dickinson or the books that Anthony thought I should have read by now. One was the Kate Chopin, which apparently Claire had brought when I was asleep. I told Miss Weston I didn't agree with the ending of *The Awakening*. Wasn't there another choice besides suicide? You could swim out, if you needed to, but shouldn't you always try to come in again?

She answered that things had changed since Chopin had written her book. Women had better choices now. She then told me about her own decision to leave Sydney to come and live in Lion's Head. She said she could have had a job in a city school by now, and be closer to home, but that sometimes it was better to leave.

'Do you miss your family?' I asked.

'Oh, I miss them. Yes, of course I do. But I had to come away to really get to know them. Now I'm so pleased I'm here, and I get to know people like you, Ted, and your father.'

'I'm glad you've stayed,' I told her.

'Well, there were other things,' she confided. 'Things didn't work out after uni. Coming to Lion's Head was good for lots of reasons.'

'It's a bit colder in Sydney, isn't it?' I asked.

Miss Weston ignored the question, as if preoccupied with those lots of reasons. Then she said, 'There was only one man in the gender studies major. Isn't that odd? I mean, is it really that hard to be interested in gender if you're a man.'

I wasn't sure.

'Men are too self-absorbed,' she concluded.

I sensed that she wanted to say something about my father, but I couldn't tell exactly what. Eric, too, had views about Dad that he'd been saving up: it didn't do for Dad to spend so much time alone. I wondered how Eric could so unknowingly speak of his own condition. From his point of view, the main thing that Dad needed was to join the bowls club.

Mostly, I sat quietly and listened, and I suppose waited; for I'd found a container for all that I wanted to say, in Anthony. I didn't know why he wanted to talk to me – I felt hopelessly ignorant when I was with him – but I liked his company very much, and accepted the role of the younger boy who needed instruction. And I recall that I got better at conversing as the days went by: Anthony was teaching me how to think from point to point, deductively, rather than from the details out. He spoke about paintings, music – mainly pop music, but also chamber music, another pleasure he kept hidden from his father, like poetry.

He shouldn't have worried, not here. Anthony's father didn't visit, and so it turned out there wasn't any need to hide the Dickinson. For the first few days, the only visitor I saw was his mother. She wouldn't sit down, and wore the distracted appearance of someone very busy or late, and yet I knew from Anthony that her life was spent watching television and reading thick romances. 'She doesn't like hospitals,' Anthony said.

'Why?'

'I don't think she ever knows what to say.'

No, but then nor did anyone else, not really. For no one knew how to talk about my accident, and I began to realise that meant we wouldn't talk about it at all. Until Claire arrived, it would remain in the sea, where it had occurred, for me and my mother to work out.

2

Those nights in the hospital, after the lights had been out for an hour, I felt as though I was back at the house, or in the water. I heard the waves, and half-dreamt that Dad had collected me early, and that we were back to our routine – the two of us, and how we'd thought about Mum in the years since she'd died.

As soon as he thought I was asleep, he'd set the needle. Sometimes at 'Un bel dì vedremo', other nights at the start of a Rossini, maybe *La Cenerentola*. The first bars counted out the opening move-ments of our evenings. By the time I was nine or ten, I understood well enough that the music had to be Romantic, for by then he'd taught me that the Romantic movement expressed the sensibility of the lonely, the sentimental; and, without being told, I knew that when he talked about those things he was describing something in himself, and something that he'd seen in me, as well.

But the effect of all that lonely beauty was different for each of us. It put him in the mood to read and write, to sit alone in the study. It made me want to leave. I'd climb out of my bedroom window and make my way down to the beach, to the accompani-ment of a score that was almost always Italian. For me, it was swimming music, just as much as it might be music for lost lovers sitting by windows. It followed me across the road to the first rise of the dune.

There weren't many trees over on our side, and you could see the house clearly. I sat as still as I could in a strip of greenery and bushes, watching my father. I knew his movements off by heart, probably because I watched them guiltily and didn't want to get caught. I could tell when he was going to come to the window by the way he stood up from the desk. I could tell when he wanted a drink, for he rose quickly and turned around. When he wanted to look out onto the street, he got up more slowly and stretched his back first.

And I knew the road the way I knew him, as an extension of the house and the way it related to the sea. I rode down it at least a dozen times every day. A shift of my weight on a tall-framed bike as I hooked left at the Lion's Head bowls club, a flick to straighten again. Eric frowning, telling me from his garden that I'd kill myself one of these days. But rushing home for my first swim, who cared about what might happen one of these days?

And then, in the evenings when Dad's records were on, giving Eric another reason to grumble, I crossed again and went out for another swim, the one that no one knew about, not even Eric. I didn't jump straight in. For a while, I sat and listened to the music. Sometimes, I waited for Dad to come to the window. He gazed out, towards my side of the street. The breeze moved the tall grass at my knees, passing by me as it took the music to our other neighbours, a street of opera-tolerants, and then over the dune and out to sea.

Eventually, I'd undress down to my shorts, fold them under a bench, and sit with my back to the house, facing the water. When a record ended or needed turning, I turned around with it. While

Dad decided what to put on next, I climbed as lightly as I could over the dune and down to the purple water of the bay.

The sea touched the grey sand of night. As quietly as possible I disrupted the stillness of it. There was that heady, first sensation of belonging as I dived under. The music was gone, muted by the bass notes of the ocean, its thudding silence. And with that, the gates to my own thoughts eased open, and I found that the Romantics were wrong.

In the sea, I wasn't the least bit lonely.

For I heard my mother's heart. That is no harder to believe now than when I was twelve and swimming out to hear it. There, along the ocean floor, its rhythm matched my own. I might have thought that it *was* merely my own, the underwater concentration of my own pulse. But there was always final evidence up at the study window, and in the music that followed me down from it. I was never the only one listening.

Anthony was up getting a glass of water. He had trouble sitting still for long, and now walked across to the window. Claire seemed used to all his restlessness, and for a moment kept her eyes on me. I blushed. Then she stood up from Anthony's chair and joined him at the window. Against the light, the arch of her back showed through her white shirt. She put her arm around his waist, below the bruises on his back, and watched the street outside.

She was shorter than him. They were in the same grade, but she was nearly a year younger, fourteen when we met properly that summer. Her thick black hair spun across his shoulder, accentuating how white Anthony was – this was unusual in a beach town, where we ignored the warnings about the sun. She turned to face me, and

I noticed, more so than before, her foreignness: whatever country her parents had brought with them was present in her cheekbones, and how they fell to her lips.

It seemed she knew a bit about me, and had questions already formed. She came over to my bed – to quiz me, apparently as her way of establishing my character. She wanted to know more about the accident, and how I'd ended up on the rough side of the Head.

'I never swim that side,' she said. 'I don't see how you could get caught there.'

I tried to boast. 'It was a rip. I was lucky to get back at all.'

'Or lucky that your dad got to you,' she replied.

'Yes.' I wondered how she'd discovered all this. 'Have you visited Anthony a lot?'

'Most days. You've been somewhere else.' I tried to calculate how I could have missed her visits. She continued, 'I've come at three-thirty ... sometimes you've been asleep. A lot. You snore.' I found her eyes to tell if she was making fun of me. The expression was more open than that. She waited for a reaction.

'Yes, I've heard that before.'

'From your dad?'

'Yes.'

'I saw him. When you were still in your own room, I mean. He sat with you for ages and sometimes left before you woke up.'

'I know.'

And then a thought that it seemed Claire had been holding in reserve: 'He looks lonely.'

'Has Anthony told you about my mum?'

'Yes. He told me that she died when you were young. It must have been an awful time.'

'I don't remember it. I was only three.'

18

'For him, I mean.' And then, 'I'm sorry.'

'But you're right. It's hardest on him.'

'No. It's just how he looks when he's waiting for you to wake up – like he's waiting for something else as well.'

'My mother's heart.' I was surprised to hear myself say it to Claire – the first time I'd put my view of him out in the open, saying what he and I had in common –

Our own ways of listening for her.

How could he fall in love, when he so obviously still listened for my mother? He did it through music; I did it in the water.

'He's already got someone,' I explained. 'My mum's still here.'

'Now?'

I met Claire's gaze and wondered if she saw how she'd hit me in the stomach. 'Right now,' I answered at last.

3

Before the accident, I swam every night that I could. And although Dad wouldn't have thanked me for it, I swam as much for his sake as for my own. I had my questions about him. About those long nights he liked to spend surrounded by books and opera. About his reluctance to give me the whole story of our life in Lion's Head, and why we'd moved here from Yorkshire. Questions that assumed there was something to discover in the way he wished for the past, and perhaps regretted it.

Their origin lay in little hints that I pocketed during the routines of each day, such as the way my teachers, during a conversation about nothing in particular, managed to talk about my father. Without ever explaining why, they would speak of him as a kind of puzzle, if not in what they actually said, then in a tone that we all recognised and reserved for the mysteries of small-town existence. It was in the way they called him 'your father' instead of 'your dad', and in the way they spoke more about him than they did others. 'Your father must notice that,' they would say to me, or, 'I expect that's something your father has spoken to you about,' be it history, the law, or some strangeness of human nature.

I wasn't yet sure what the pieces of the puzzle were, or which piece was missing. He'd started life here as a lawyer. Now he was the magistrate, but still a foreigner, and still a widower. The whole town knew those things, and I supposed that these parts of his identity added up to a suite of questions for those who watched him. To me, it seemed there was more to know because that's how he wanted it to seem, what he quietly implied. In a town that liked to leave all its doors unlocked, he wanted certain doors to remain closed, even with me. It didn't trouble me the way it troubled the town. I'd grown up with it.

It was why I went swimming at night, in any case. Everyone was hoping for a glimpse of my mother, but what was clear to me, if not others, was that the glimpse of her that they saw in the stillness behind his smile lay also under the white light on the water.

For some, the most pressing matter was my father's decision to remain single. It amazed me how doggedly our friends returned to the topic of marriage time and again, as though one day the oddness of his still being single would be cracked, and he'd be made understandable. They said that he and I should have a woman's care, as though it were the 1950s. They insisted that there was no reason for us not to have a woman around. He was still handsome, even the sort of man who became more handsome with age. They thought he must have been in his early forties.

And in his way he was charming, too. I'd seen it. He flattered the ladies of Lion's Head with a very light kind of teasing that wasn't at all normal in town. Once, when Miss Weston walked past our house on her way to school, she brought him a cake. She said it was to thank him for some books he'd donated to the school. But for some Mondays in a row, she repeated the gesture and it began to look like a routine – although she said these treats were just extras from her baking the day before. Eventually I understood it properly.

For a while I thought she might have a chance: her cakes weren't very good, but she was so well read. She talked about the Brontës, who she said, like us, were from the North. She said it brought an identity, a sensibility.

But it came to nothing. Not even the Brontë sisters could do it. A sympathetic expression that Miss Weston shot at me on one of her visits predicted that my father would never let anyone in, not even the young, pretty and well-read ones, who for his sake might have broken a previous rule against baking for men. It wasn't Miss Weston's fault, or the Brontës', or the fault of the other ladies of Lion's Head. The fault lay with love itself, and how it refused to be calmed. At least so I thought. For this reason, my father was never able to encourage the gaze of another. Too fast, he looked away, and returned his eyes to the one we'd search for at night. I saw that he was still in love with my mother, and I loved him all the more for it.

So, with no locals to draw him out of himself, and explain him properly to the rest of the town, our neighbours were left instead with their curiosity. They shared it around, and often I was able to join it to my own. They gave me clues that supported my own thoughts about him.

And once, when two of our neighbours stopped on their evening walk and looked up to the house, failing to see me sitting in the shadows, they unwittingly told me something he hadn't yet mentioned. They stood close to me, and the streetlights caught the sides of their faces.

One said that she'd heard that my mother had died in a swimming accident in Yorkshire.

Yes, that was right, answered the other.

When they were out of sight I walked down to the sea, dizzy with finally understanding why I wanted to swim all the time.

I dived beneath the surface, and listened for her heart again. And I promised I would swim as far out as she needed me to.

By the time Dad got back from Sydney, I'd told the story to Anthony and Claire – in instalments, a story of how I'd ended up in hospital. Anthony asked more and more questions, until I felt like I was one of his books, or one of the titles that Dad brought back from Sydney for my birthday. He said to open them early. I unwrapped *Robinson Crusoe*, *Treasure Island* and *Dracula* – early tales of Northerners adrift, and one of a vampire who ended up in our hometown, Whitby.

For Anthony and Claire I'd said in plain words that Dad was a widower, and that I'd never really known my mother, but that I held on as dearly as I could to my barest memories of her. And I confided in them that my father would only ever love her. He'd never be able to put our earlier life in Whitby behind him. But although I was sure everyone knew this about him, I felt awkward when Dad visited next, as though I'd betrayed him again. I'd had a swimming accident, and now I was telling strangers about his heart.

He didn't notice. He approved of the Dickinson on my bedside table, and I felt this almost as an approval of Anthony and the confidences that were springing up between us. 'You're reading poetry at last,' Dad said.

'It's my age,' I replied.

He wondered whether there was a girl to whom he could attribute the interest. 'The nurses are pretty.'

For a moment, I enjoyed his confusion, and a flicker of mischief that was rare between us. 'Yes,' I said. 'They've been asking about you, too.'

He smiled. 'Then I should get out while I can.'

I introduced him to Anthony. I was nervous, as though I were introducing a rival. Neither of them noticed that, either. They talked about the Dickinson, and the other North American poets that Dad liked.

They got along well, which surprised me: my father didn't take to people so quickly. And something else suddenly appeared. I saw it and understood it: a space between Dad and me that Anthony was walking into. While the two of them sat and talked – Anthony on the bed and my father in the chair beside it – I knew from then on that I'd relate best to my father when I was in the company of others. With Anthony, and also Claire.

4

Strangely, not everyone fell in love with Claire that summer. It seemed that there were scores of people in town, even those within our small, ocean-side parts of Lion's Head and its skirt of estates, who could have watched her walk to Anthony's bed as passively as they watched a stranger stroll from the surf club to the sea. She wasn't one of the girls you heard boys talking about, included neither among the ones thought too beautiful to approach, nor those too approachable to be beautiful, in the way we imagined things should go. Perhaps it was because she was a boarder at her school, and less visible than the girls who came down to the beach in the afternoons. Or perhaps it was because, like Anthony, she was ever so slightly to the side of it all anyway.

In the days that followed, the large bandage was finally replaced with a smaller one, and I was usually around when Claire made her visit. She always spoke with the directness of our first meeting – about the bandaging, where we lived, school. She wanted to know about Miss Weston, who'd once taught Anthony too, when he was still at primary school. Claire noticed that she was always leaving at around the time Dad arrived.

'Do you mean, is Miss Weston trying to win over Dad?'

'Yes.'

'She still has to bring me books; she wants me to be ready for high school next year. But I think she leaves when she does because she's stopped trying.'

'That's a shame,' Claire said.

She didn't revisit the topic of my mother. All the same, that first conversation remained contained by the others, and animated her, I'm sure, on the day she decided that the three of us should break out of hospital. She said she wanted to show me something.

Claire had been planning it: she unfolded two sets of Anthony's clothes. I didn't ask her how she'd got them. Apparently, it was self-evident that she would know how.

I waited for her to speak. 'Just put them on,' she said.

The children's ward was on the ground floor. We could leave by the fire exit.

'Let me try the door first,' said Claire. 'I'll just say I leant on it if it goes off.'

She pressed her side against a silver handle, and pushed the door open. The alarm didn't go. In front of us a cement ramp wrapped the wall, back across the windows of the ward we were meant to be in.

'Where are we going?' asked Anthony.

'I'll tell you later. We have to get past this window.' Claire, the one who didn't need to hide, crouched under the window frame and shuffled to the other side.

'I can't crouch,' I whispered across the bridge now formed between us. 'The stitches.'

And so Claire walked back. 'Come with me,' she said. We walked past the window, in our clothes two Anthonys trying to appear casual, expecting to see a quiet ward. I looked left. Half-a-dozen children were at the window, watching our every move.

I waved at them. 'I think we're busted.'

'Just keep walking,' said Anthony, and we were gone.

We crossed a hot car park, and a traffic island of brown grass and low palms. Waited for the traffic to clear. 'Thank you for bringing me along,' I said.

Claire smiled in reply. 'Just wait.'

It was Saturday, market day. As we walked towards my school, the side of the road became more crowded with parked cars. We were shadowed by a slow convoy of people trying to find a parking spot.

'Does your dad ever come?' asked Claire.

'No. He grows his own vegies.'

'He'd like my father, then.'

Anthony and I knew some of the same people, for my teachers were his old teachers. They asked him how high school was going, and looked at Claire in that way old teachers have, as though they've seen something they predicted years before. Anthony told me that he loved his English and art teachers, but that everyone else thought he was too argumentative.

Claire said, 'Anthony thinks people hate him, when all they want is for him to chill.'

Anthony smiled. 'It's your day,' he said to her. 'Of course I'll be chilled.'

Her day, I now discovered, was the sudden appearance of Greece in the middle of the Saturday markets, and her parents' stall of olives, tomatoes and citrus fruits.

'This is Ted,' Claire called over the market noise.

'Hallo, Ted,' her father called back. 'I'm Nikolas. Claire's mother is the one cutting up watermelon. Have some. Christina, bring over for the boys.'

27

Christina's temples shone with sweat. As she came over from the cutting table at the back, she glanced at Claire, an expression you'd have to be blind not to understand. *You have two boys following you around now*, it said. *And we were just getting used to Anthony.*

She waited for Nikolas to do something, although I can't think what there was to be done, even then. His response to Claire's new admirer was simply to pretend that I wasn't one – or that everyone was, and so it made no great difference. Claire ignored it all. She crossed to her parents' side of the counter, and reached over it with the tray of watermelon for us to taste.

'It's delicious,' she said, while her mother went back to the cutting table, as if accepting her daughter's fate and her own defeat.

'Leave some for our customers,' Christina said to Claire.

5

When he was discharged from the hospital, Anthony left behind the Dickinson, whether I wanted it or not. Inside it, he'd transcribed words that were as oddly confidential as our first conversation had been. A line from one of the poems: *The soul selects her own society.*

Three weeks after the accident, and a few days before Christmas, my father collected me from the hospital and we drove back to our side of Lion's Head. He'd been kind to me in the hospital, but during the drive I felt something that he'd been waiting to express. His voice sounded sore – an extra strain in the wind.

This built as we got nearer to home.

I couldn't face him then: I didn't want to see his face. But this made him angrier. He didn't speak until we got to the front steps, when he pressed me inside and towards my room. 'Wait for me,' he said.

For an hour, I sat there, at the end of my bed. When he came back, it was getting dark.

He stood at the door. 'You nearly died. Do you know that?'

'Yes, Dad.'

'Why would you be so damned stupid?'

I had no explanation for that, and sat staring at the hands in my lap, hands that I always felt were such poor imitations against his. He left again, stomping down the hall to the kitchen and then making a big show of getting dinner ready, pulling the pans out heavily and knocking them against the cupboards. That was when I knew he'd forgiven me – when the anger had turned into a huff.

He came back and told me that dinner was nearly ready. He added, 'I'm sorry I'm so angry. Come and eat.'

'It's okay, Dad,' I replied to his back as I followed it along the hall. He turned to me, and put his hand out for mine. I said, 'It's my fault. I'm sorry for swimming so far on my own.'

'You frightened me. I thought you were too far out for me to help you.'

'I know.'

All of a sudden, we were both very hungry. He cooked perch in butter and garlic, and then served it with boiled potatoes. As always, on the side of his plate were lightly fried onions and tomatoes, and a wedge of bright yellow mustard.

'It's really good fish, Dad,' I said, even though we had the same thing every second night.

'Very fresh,' he answered.

I then asked him a question that I couldn't usually have asked, I suppose as much as anything because it was a question that had gone unasked for so long: 'How did Mum die?'

He put down his cutlery. 'She drowned,' he said. He watched me nod. 'Did you know that?'

'I heard someone talk about it.'

This stopped him for a moment – the reminder that there was a life outside the house, one in which we were discussed and puzzled over. 'Of course you've heard talk. That's bad on my part. I'm sorry.'

He continued to himself, 'Other people told you.' He examined me. 'Who did tell you?'

This wasn't the moment to tell Dad about my night swims. 'I can't remember,' I said.

'It was always hard to know the best time to talk to you about it.'

'I know.'

Again, he held my hand. Again, the lovely sensation of insignificance at feeling mine against his. 'Your mother drowned,' he repeated. 'There. Does it help you understand why I'm angry? Why it frightened me?'

'Yes.' But I was surprised to hear him mention fear a second time.

'Can you promise not to do that again, to swim out on your own like that?'

'Yes,' I said. I wanted more fish. He hadn't really cooked enough.

'It's a promise,' he said.

'I promise, Dad. I don't want to swim anymore.'

'Do you want something else to eat?' he asked, seeing me watching his plate. He was a slow eater.

I nodded.

'I'll put on some eggs, then,' he said, and pushed himself from the table. 'You're not getting my fish.' He was smiling at last. 'Not after the hell you've put me through.'

'How did it happen?' I asked. 'Did Mum get caught out?'

He moved his coffee pot to the side and stood by the stove. 'I'm not sure how it happened,' he answered. His voice, like his hands, cupped a greater significance than mine. But he added a severe note, a reminder of what I'd promised: 'Plenty of good swimmers drown. Your mum was one of those. She must have been unlucky.'

I wondered why he wouldn't say more. 'She always swam? When she was a girl?'

'Yes.'

'I remember her,' I said. 'I remember her dark hair. Her curls – thick, curly hair.'

He walked back to the table with my plate. He'd cooked three eggs for me. 'No,' he said. 'That wasn't your mother. You're remembering your aunt Lillie, my sister. She took care of you in those days, after your mother died.'

I watched his face, waiting for more. Could I really have mis-remembered something like that?

'Why don't we have any pictures of Mum?' I asked.

He didn't answer straight away. For a while, I didn't think he would. He finished his fish in silence, and by the time he was done I thought he was going to go back to the study to work, as he usually did after dinner. He stood up and walked that way. But then I heard him unlock a drawer in his desk, a sequence of sounds I'd heard before, other nights when I was meant to be asleep, and he came back with a slim envelope. From it, he drew a black-and-white photograph. He gave it to me carefully by the edges, against his palms, as one holds a record.

The picture was the size of a postcard, with a white border. In it, a young woman and a child: my mother leaning against a stone wall that was dark against a white day, or perhaps the wash of over-exposure. In the background, a faint outline of the entrance to Whitby harbour. Me sitting on the wall, and Mum's arm around me, her hand across my shirt. She was wearing a cardigan, unbuttoned at the top; the dark collar of a white blouse showed underneath.

'That's her and me?'

'Yes, that's you and your mother. What do you think?'

'I think she's beautiful.'

But not in the way I'd remembered. Dad was right. I'd been thinking of someone else, his sister Lillie. I followed his eyes, and for a moment tried to find myself not in the child on the wall, but in the gaze that my mother offered the camera. Had she looked at me in this way? What I saw most clearly was happiness. And my own happiness: that was the trace light that suddenly formed around my dim sense of her, and re-lit a memory of her movement around me, her hand against the back of my neck as we walked along a wet path.

'Yes, your mother was beautiful,' Dad said. 'Almost too beautiful.'

He'd said this before. But I didn't know what it meant to be too beautiful. Spoken by my father, it sounded like a condition in law.

'Did she always have straight hair?' I asked.

'Her hair was straight, yes. And very fine.'

After he took the photograph back, he asked me to explain why I'd been swimming out so far. It was my chance to tell him that for over a year I'd known that she drowned, and that I thought that if I swam for long enough she might join me in the deep, on the seabed.

But the idea of saying it out loud made it seem like such nonsense, not because I didn't believe in it or because I didn't think he'd understand, but because it would have meant explaining something that had for so long existed privately, as my side of the nights that we spent divided by his opera collection. We were both too shy for that.

So, instead of answering his question, I said, 'I wish she was still alive. I miss her.'

'Me, too, Ted,' he said, and let me off.

*

That evening, he expanded on a fact I'd heard in the passing remarks of our neighbours. My mother, Isabel, had died when I was three, a year before we moved to Lion's Head. Her death had prompted our migration to Australia. He said she was in Scarborough now – her ashes were kept in a town she'd loved during her childhood, a place of holidays and the seaside, but also close to Scarborough beach, where she'd drowned.

Most of her family was from Durham, a university town a little inland from his and my birthplace, Whitby. He said hers had been a family of academics. His family's background was in fishing. He was proud of this, but also of being the first to reach beyond a long history on the North Sea trawlers and into the path of someone like her. They were different: he was there to get ahead, while she often learnt things for their own sake, spending hours on her own.

'Do you mean reading?' I said.

'Yes, she read a lot, hours and hours every day. Mostly by the river that runs through Durham – there's so many places to sit there. That's how I met her. I started talking to a beautiful girl who was sitting on her own, reading by the river. For some reason, I didn't think anything of interrupting her.'

'Did you fall in love that day?'

'It was before then.'

He was ready to stop, but I kept on. 'What happened before then?'

'We didn't know each other, but we were in the same literature class. She had strong ideas, especially about books and what they might or might not be saying about the world. I didn't. Or, I didn't have as strong ideas as hers. I liked that about her. It suited the way she spoke, the way she spent all that time on her own sorting things out, like she was getting ready for something grand. Do you follow what I mean?'

He was speaking more to himself than to me, and my understanding wasn't really needed. But I nodded in agreement, so that he'd go on. 'She seemed older than me, even though I was the older one, because she didn't ever hold back, and already she knew so much more than I did. She was soaked in her parents' knowledge. She didn't realise it, but it was as clear as day to me.

'I'm not sure how much I took in. She would talk about medieval romances, or the use of imagery in Sidney, or how Wordsworth might or might not have reclined before he put pen to paper. I didn't care terribly much about these things, but I liked that they mattered to her, and I liked it that she was serious. It made her beautiful. That's why I sat next to her on the bench that day.' He joked with himself: 'She needed interrupting by someone like me.'

'I wish I'd known her.'

'You did. You knew her.' I wanted to hold him when he said that, but I didn't want him to stop talking. 'And she knew you. You were hers. You were her boy.'

With that, he remembered again that he was meant to be talking to me. He said, 'When she passed away, I felt very bad, very bad about losing her. Sometimes making a fresh start is the only chance you have in these situations. I decided not to spend forever trying to make sense of what we'd lost. I know it's not the same for you. You need her, and I should give you more of her. Tell you more. But there was no point in coming out to Australia if we were going to spend our lives thinking of Whitby. That's why I haven't put the picture out.'

He took it back to the desk, and I sensed then that there was still more to ask, parts concealed. When he returned, he said, 'We can look at it again whenever you like.'

*

35

I felt I would be searching for her forever, and for what might be unlocked in the moments when my father spoke like this. I thought I could see her black hair as she leant forward to kiss me. A fragment of place: a street of red buildings, a stroke of yellow light against wet windows, her steps along the pavement, an overcoat that swung at her ankles, my hand finding hers in her pocket.

6

Dad had always called me Ted, and so that's how everyone knew me; I suppose it was better and easier than Theodore. But that's what people called him – Theodore, or more often Mr Haigh. He said it was Mum's idea to give me his name, and joked that he would have preferred a less cumbersome handle for both of us.

I never found it easy to ask him to bring her photo out, but now and then I pressed him to fetch it. I tried to replace my early impressions of Lillie with this, the correct image of Mum, and beneath the image tried to find a memory of us by the ocean wall.

He didn't enjoy these moments. They seemed to cost him more than they gave me. I had never seen my father cry, but once when he held the photograph he put his fingers to his mouth in a way I hadn't seen before. I'd made a promise, and I would keep it. It was a crucial one for him, and each time I got to the beach, and looked towards the surf club and its warning signs, I read them as reminders of the photograph, and its effect on him.

He now tried a little too hard to be light-hearted. I wouldn't get out of school as easily next time, he told me. And he said there was a reason he'd been reading Greene: the high school had finally agreed with him and set *The Quiet American*. I'd be studying it in the coming year. We could read it together, he said. A joint project.

But from then on we began to read things differently. That was what happened in the space of those weeks in the hospital, and in the space between being hauled out of the sea and onto the rocks and telling Claire why I'd ended up on them.

After the stitches healed and the cut was completely closed, he offered to take me swimming. I replied that I'd prefer not to go in the water again.

'That's not how to deal with this,' he said. 'Are you scared?'

'No.'

'What is it, then?'

'I'm not going in.'

He put his hand on my arm. For a moment, I thought he was angry again. He said, 'You're alright now. You got away with it. Don't forget that.'

There would be a scar, that was all. One that would remember itself as tightness across the skin, more noticeable on hot days or if I walked a lot. By the end of my first weeks in high school, touching it had become a habit, a kind of companion. My stomach was very flat and the mark was raised, a dull and uneven red line that was uglier than the gash it had replaced. I traced it with my thumb, and with my hands I learnt its line, as the tongue learns the lines of a worn-down tooth.

I thought of Claire breaking us out of the hospital, and wondered what it had all meant – her ability to take me from thinking too much inside to being out in the street, eating fruit in the mid-morning sun.

At night, I lay in bed and felt the escape all over again, and felt

38

also a desire that grew around the scar, part of how it healed. I wanted to have Claire there, asking questions while Anthony stood at the window. To have her distance, how self-contained she could be, but also those moments when she demanded to know something, and revealed the questions she'd been forming while she was away. When she watched my father and me, as though we were cracks that ran across adjoining windows.

I watched out for her through mine, across the lawn and the path that once witnessed my escapes from opera lessons and their light residue of cigar smoke. When she didn't come, when the fantasy of an unexpected visit dulled into reality, I let her in through another window, and I lay instead as close to the memory of her as I could. I touched her lower back, and felt her hand on mine.

7

Dad had bought our place straight after we moved from Yorkshire, but although he paid for it outright it never possessed him any more than it did on the day of the purchase. He said firmly that he wasn't ever going to return to England, but I'd begun to see that he wasn't ever going to be quite here, either. He tended the garden. He painted a section of wall or a room every few years. But otherwise his only improvement was to rearrange the place around his books and his record player.

After I came back from hospital, the place felt unbearably still. His study was the exception, but only because it so strongly bore the character of his books and papers, the life of his mind: he made a clearing among the columns of materials that he was reading and working on. It wasn't something that he did for the house; it was something he did for himself, or even to escape a part of himself.

And he took the escape with him wherever we went. If ever we travelled by road, on country drives we took each year or when he was required on circuit, he brought a backseat of reading materials excerpted from his various projects: cases and court matters, but also books on music, poetry and civil rights – which he believed were the three components of understanding how people got along.

When we got back from these trips, I always noticed the flavour of smoke in the rooms where my father spent his time: it was by far the most permanent mark that he left on the house. The study; the annex at the back of the house where he kept more of his books; and the kitchen where he drank coffee, and where he would turn up as an unexpected visitor, his cigar smoke trailing behind him – these three rooms accepted the smoke into their walls. If it were possible I think they would have captured the music as well, for he hummed and smoked constantly as he walked between rooms. I watched and felt I understood more now.

Unwittingly, perhaps, he'd turned our house into a chapel in its final decline, a place to worship what he regarded as real: the law, the work of the mind, but always most crucially the voice. The voice was what made opera interesting, and what made listening the greatest art of all: the tonal range of a brilliant singer was not only up and down the scale, but across it as well. He taught me that the best voices were cross-hatched with meaning.

Music, he said, was God for the materialist, the humanist. His record player sat on a side table, on the only part of the house that was properly level. It was as fixed as an altar, bracketed on one side by his office and on the other the hallway to the annex. When he put a record on, the ceilings and the windows lifted enough to let the ocean come in.

It was just the two of us, a point he stressed more often after the accident. He had to take care of me, as I was to take care of him. He liked to sit and talk to me until I got too tired to listen. Composers' lives, absurd librettos and legal histories were his pet topics for these discussions. He thought I should know opera and now assumed that I would want to be a lawyer; I was spared none of his obsessions. He said the kernel of most problems lay in the old

41

world. The solution to all of them lay in the voice, in the willingness to talk and listen.

I loved these conversations, not because of his philosophies or what he taught me, but because his own voice was so rich, and such a beautiful instrument. Afterwards, when it was time for me to sleep, he closed the door behind him. Instead of listening to his voice, I heard his chair creak as he pushed against its back. When it creaked again, half an hour later, the sound was followed by footsteps along the wooden boards of the hallway, and he was standing at my door, listening to check I was asleep. And then he returned to his Beogram, with its rosewood plinth and a sound to rouse the sea.

Such was the strange, dislocated world of tenderness and absence that I would have liked Anthony and Claire to make whole. I was sure their presence could enliven the rooms in our house, just as they'd brought the light into the hospital ward – the certainty that, under even the deepest seriousness, life always holds the possibility of a surprise. Olives on a quiet Saturday.

I wanted their close friendship. It was an infatuation.

I wanted to phone Anthony to tell him that he and Dickinson were right: the soul did select her own company, and my soul had selected them. It had selected them to take the stillness out of a house that needed more than music and commemoration, to take the stillness out of a father who didn't want to fall in love again – maybe, after all, Claire was right to ask why not. Maybe I was wrong to love that he didn't.

But for some time after I got home Anthony and Claire sailed into a middle distance that reflected, I suppose, our age differences: they were both a grade ahead; Claire was a year older, Anthony almost two. I saw them around, for they stood apart from the life of Lion's Head as clearly as white sails stand clear of sand islands behind them. But, like those white sails, they didn't appear to move very much. They existed out there in a separate channel. Only when you looked back to watch them again, did you notice that they'd changed.

They were an old-fashioned couple. Like everyone else they smoked, but in a more careful way: they sat at the bench near the old cinema, with their legs crossed, leaning forward and talking, often arguing. They could have been waiting for the doors to open, or for the 1920s to end – their separateness placed them decades in the past, and from afar they were silent movie stars. Sometimes I saw them from the other side of the river as I rode into town. As I neared, we waved to each other. But they didn't call me over, and for my part I thought it rude to interrupt couples sitting on benches. Perhaps if it had been Claire on her own I would have stopped. I would have done what Dad had done for Mum, and persuaded her to stop reading and talk instead.

In a small town like ours, the standard modifications were to cars, motorbikes, and sometimes even bikes, which, like the locals, were got up to appear bigger and rougher than they really were. Anthony and Claire tackled their uniforms. Instead of bringing themselves forward into the fast life of adulthood – short skirts and top buttons undone – they adopted a more distant style. Anthony wore trousers and fitted shirts, and Claire was one of the girls who left their skirts long. It was partly nostalgia. But also, in those days, I think it was their pleasure in formality, which in a way stood for the city and foreignness – a future that would take them into the greater world.

*

When I saw them, I thought again on that odd notion of some things in life being too beautiful. Too beautiful, I wondered, for either me or Anthony, or too beautiful to be accepted? At that age, most of us admired only sweetness, but Claire's beauty lay somewhere further out, beyond the bright, brown skin and coastal freshness of other girls. They were prettier than her. Her thick hair was in no sense Pacific; it belonged entirely to the Adriatic and to Greece. And if she was sensual, her body was also lazier than those around her, absorbing the light and energy into itself. I would watch her, trying to catch her eye. When she finally looked at me, shocked me with her stare, I thought that beauty – or this quality of being *too* beautiful – might lie in the moments when she decided I still needed figuring out. Beauty wasn't only where the eye rested. Beauty lay in its demands.

It took me the best part of two years to heed those demands, and to say anything much beyond a greeting. But gradually, the age difference between us, which had seemed to measure such a wide arc of understanding when I was turning thirteen, became less important. There were sympathies that mattered more than age.

I heard from others that Anthony and Claire wanted to be artists. In Lion's Head, this meant that they were part of a light comedy that the town constructed around them – their pretentiousness and their hopes of leaving. But they didn't seem to care. That was what marked you out as an artist, I thought: you were willing to show your hand and risk seeming gauche. And so I took my chances one afternoon, sitting near them at the side of our school athletics carnival. Claire had come down from her school to watch.

I called out hello but stayed awhile with a group of friends. They seemed happy on their own, Anthony in sunglasses and his own

44

version of the school sports uniform. It was obvious he wasn't going to compete.

He waved back, but didn't call me over. I turned away and wondered what I could say to them. Nothing came, but when my friends said they were going up to the shop for lunch, I stayed on and at last shifted over towards Anthony and Claire's spot on the grass.

'How have you been?' she said. 'Sit here with us.'

I shuffled further across, next to her. Anthony said, 'Hi, Ted.'

'Have you been in an event today?' asked Claire.

'High jump,' I said. 'And long jump. And hurdles.' But I wanted to move the conversation to art. I doubted that they cared all that much about sport. 'You're both painting a lot, aren't you?'

'Trying,' she said. 'School's getting a bit crazy.'

'I won a book about Streeton,' I replied, awkwardly. 'I'm reading about the Australian impressionists.'

I thought I was being quite impressive. But Anthony didn't want to talk about art, not directly. He seemed instead to want to pick up where we'd left off at the hospital. He said, 'It's funny how people meet when they discover something that they need in another person.'

'I met you because you wanted me to read poems,' I answered.

'You must have needed poetry, then.'

'And you?'

He didn't tell me. He asked, 'How did you go in the hurdles?'

'I came sixth of six.'

They laughed. I spent that afternoon with them, and over time more and more afternoons. If it was true that we needed many things from others, the more we talked the more I sensed that those things were also out of reach, and out of town, and that perhaps

45

what the three of us needed most was a shared belief in that other-world that would one day supply everything we longed for.

To begin with, the future existed only as an excited conversation on the beach. One afternoon, the three of us met after school. For the two hours that Claire was allowed out of school we sat on the dune in front of my house and talked. We rushed through the impossibilities – collected them as diamonds to be spent in the years to come.

Anthony and Claire would do nothing but paint. We'd get to meet our heroes, not the living ones but the artists who'd come and gone on the same streets. We'd meet them along their faded footprints, in Sydney, and then in Paris and London and New York. We wouldn't stop until we knew their footsteps as our own.

A vast world lay beyond our conquering. We didn't know London or Paris, and that's what made them seem like the future. There was no familiarity, no streets we had ridden a thousand times. Only those impressions left by the great. Wasn't that almost as good as art itself?

'But will you do it?' I asked Claire. 'Will you leave after school?'

She was adamant. 'I can't spend my life on a farm, like my parents have.'

'You couldn't stay here?'

'No. Nor can you.'

8

No one would ever have called Lion's Head a showy town, but nor was it hostile to the arrival of something new, as long as the new made sure to camouflage any well-meaning intentions or sense of improvement it might bring. The town had accepted better coffee and café culture some years before. Now, in the new millennium, it seemed you could expect to overhear as many conversations about red wine and the dominance of shiraz as about cricket.

Anthony and I spent more time together at school; I learnt that he had his views about what the town needed next. We were all so fat, he said. He knew that Lion's Head was not going to stop eating fatty meats, and so, instead of a campaign for vegetarianism, he advertised tai chi to run at the Rotary park next to the surf club. It was just before the summer holidays. Claire and I helped him put up the posters around town, but neither of us expected a crowd. We thought we would be Anthony's only customers.

The price would get them in, he said. Your first session was free, and after that you could come for a gold-coin donation. His profits would go to an animal shelter on the outskirts of town, next door to the tile suppliers. And though his cause was probably something the town could have accepted, Anthony left his altruism as unspoken as his aims.

I trusted the town on many things, but I wasn't sure they were ready for Anthony as a small businessman. And yet on the first day, he managed to attract four teachers, including Miss Weston, who was the youngest there, and six of his mother's friends. And it went from there, until by the fourth week some thirty middle-aged ladies, dressed in tights and singlets, stood in an obedient semi-circle around Anthony, waiting for instruction. It seemed that none of them cared about the rumours about Anthony that circulated, and that even I, his friend, had started to hear – that he might be gay, on drugs; that his father was a terrible bully. The mayor's wife, when she joined the group, seemed to agree that what mattered most was getting to spend a Wednesday afternoon outside. And how much better they felt for it.

Claire and I weren't really needed. One afternoon, we walked around to the other side of the surf club, which stood on the isthmus between the two beaches, behind the headland. I sat with her while she drew the rocks and the corridor of pine trees that stood as an honour guard to the Head.

'Would you like to be on your own?' I said.

'No.'

'I could get us a drink.'

She glanced up from her sketchpad. 'Aren't you listening?'

Later, after class when the ladies went upstairs to the balcony bar of the surf club for a white wine, Anthony joined us on the beach. Claire and I were talking. He pulled out his journal so that he could make his own drawings, and sat a little behind us, away to the side.

'Are you going to show us?' I asked.

'Can't you see I'm deliberately not interrupting you,' he joked in reply. 'Leave me in peace!'

Claire had been talking to me about Anthony when he arrived; maybe he'd sensed it and for that reason stayed back. She'd said that I made him happier, and made her feel better about him, more relaxed. She and Anthony had once sat on the end of my hospital bed and demanded answers from me. Now, as suddenly, they seemed to want me there to hold them closer together, rather as the isthmus held the two beaches behind the Head – even if our talk was most often about getting away.

That evening, I shared with my father new theories about art and the possibility of meaningful escape. Maybe that was a mistake, for I knew that at the heart of his exile from England lay an impossible, failed one.

But he replied that there was something to what we said. The best minds searched for what they didn't know and hadn't experienced, because so much else was entertainment. We didn't need any more of that, he thought. But he added this: you usually find what you most need right in front of you.

'What about the spirit?' I asked. 'What about if the soul wants more?' I was ready to quote Anthony on this. 'Don't you think sometimes we're drawn to things we don't understand, but that we need? Isn't that why it's important to leave?'

He replied, 'Don't you think the soul is perfectly measured by the people we love? I think if you don't find the spirit reflected there, you're going about love the wrong way.'

Yes. But there was magic in flight, too – in the unreachable.

'Why do you want magic?' he said. 'Are you in love?'

'I'm not sure.'

He wanted to tease me out of my seriousness. He put his hand on my forehead and looked at me closely. A medical examination. But I was determined to be stubborn, and I didn't return his stare. He went on, 'I've read that falling in love feels like magic, or chaos, for some people. I think they must be mad. Or they're reading the wrong poets.'

'You think poets are the reason people go mad? Wasn't that how you felt about Mum?'

He'd taken his hand from my forehead. 'Some poets go on and on about the moon. That's dangerous. Very likely to produce madness in the impressionable reader.'

'Well, that's me.'

'Wait and see. My guess is that the chaos ends. At some point, you're sure, and then you stop thinking about escape.'

'Is that how it goes?'

'When you're sure about whether or not you're in love, let me know. I'll prescribe a poet closer to the ground.' He put his arm over my shoulder. 'We'll keep you a safe distance from the moon.'

I laughed at last, and told Dad I would be alright. If he was worried about Anthony and Claire's influence, he never said it, and insisted to me that Anthony could stay over whenever he wanted. They liked each other – their first impressions of each other had been right – and sometimes would take it in turns to tease me. They both thought I was too serious, even if they both knew that I was, in fact, the least preoccupied of us.

Anthony took to visiting every second or third night. He wanted to get away from his father, and so he talked to mine instead. I liked to listen, and I didn't interrupt. I wasn't always being ponderous, even if that's how it appeared. But sometimes I preferred to think about

Claire and what she might be doing. About how difficult it might be to break her out of the boarding school one night and bring her down to the beach, as she had brought me to the markets that day.

Anthony knew much more about my father's public world than I did, or all the thinking behind it, at least. They could talk about history, about Dworkin and Hayek and American legal realism, and I could see how relieved Dad was to have someone questioning the role of the law, someone to argue with. He accepted the chance to hear Anthony's lectures on peaceful anarchy, better farming practices, whatever came up each night – that the world was burning itself and that no legal system could ever keep up with what lay ahead. If they both knew that Anthony's opinions sounded more like album titles than arguments, it didn't matter. The point was dissent, and the eventual possibility of change. That was exciting.

For his part, Dad warned Anthony that one day he might have to stop fighting and come up with something constructive. 'Maybe in your paintings,' Dad told him. 'It's always possible to produce something useful in art. Something more than statements.'

Anthony made fun of himself, and said of course he had his views and always would. But he wasn't blind to the obvious. 'The most constructive thing in the world is a woman's body,' he said, 'and that's why it's the most beautiful thing, too.'

Dad looked at me, and for a moment the two of them waited for me to say something. But now that the conversation had finally caught up with my own thoughts, I tried to push the two of them back to their abstractions, their masculine deductions. 'Beauty is when the high and the low are equal,' I offered.

'Claire's only high,' said Anthony, refusing the bait.

*

51

At the end of the night, Dad let us take a scotch down to the beach. We both carried down glasses but very different conversations that we wanted to have. I needed to talk about Claire, not whether she was beautiful or not, but simpler things like how she and Anthony had met and fallen in love, and what her life had been like before then.

'I love your dad,' said Anthony instead. 'Almost as much as I love you.'

I told him to light us cigarettes, and we sat drinking. There was a stalemate, for neither of us would return to the other's conversation. I didn't want to figure Dad out, not then. I didn't think I'd ever know what happened in Whitby before we came. Maybe Anthony thought he wouldn't ever know Claire as she'd been before he met her. For once, I could refer him to a poem, 'Maiden Name' by Larkin. He said he would read it.

He put his arm around me. 'Thank God for this.'

'This?'

'For having somewhere I'm not made to feel horrible about myself.'

'Is that what your dad does?'

'Well, he hates me. Or maybe he just hates everything. It's worse for Mum. She doesn't have anywhere to go, like I do.'

'Could she get away? The two of you.'

'She's too scared to leave him.'

I wanted to ask more, but Anthony said not to. There was no point in going over it. We got tipsy quickly, and then cold. I gazed solemnly at the moon, and decided it had too many admirers and deserved none. The moon was an idiot. There were hundreds of girls I liked: Kirsty, Angie, Julie.

'They all end in -ee,' Anthony observed.

'Fuck off,' I said.

'And they're all short, Ted. You can't fall in love with short girls. You're too tall.'

'Shut up. I'll fall in love with whoever I want.'

'Prove it.'

And perhaps that was the moment to tell him. 'You don't know her,' I muttered.

'There,' he said, 'nearly the truth. I know her, and I don't.' He ran down our dune, out of sight of the house and onto the beach, past the shadows thrown by porch lights and towards the white light at the water's edge.

'Come back!' I yelled.

'No!' he called, and so I ran down after him. I didn't want him swimming in the dark. It was dangerous. I tackled him in the shallows. Dad's music was going. I think we wanted to disturb him. But it was breezy, and there was no way he'd hear us, no matter how loudly we shouted.

If I didn't catch Anthony after school, most afternoons I went next door to Eric's garden and we would talk about his repairs to the dune – trying to hold back the erosion of the dune wall. Or about the fishing, which was his other main recreation. I'd begun to notice that his place wasn't really a house. It didn't have foundations, but sat like an over-large construction office on old bricks and timbers. The grass stopped growing as it neared the edge of this hut, abashed by low shadows.

'Is this actually your house?' I asked him once.

'Well, I don't own it, if that's what you mean.' Eric was what he called a 'permanent temporary', and he said that there was nothing better. Don't get stuck, he warned.

And yet he seemed completely stuck, even if only temporarily. I went inside once. Once was enough. He wanted to show me his record collection, which I think he'd long hoped to present as a rival to my father's. Mainly, it was Dizzy Gillespie and Count Basie, big-band legends and dance-hall favourites. The only *real* music. He said, 'I don't play them as loudly as your dad. I'm a much more considerate neighbour.'

'Maybe that's a good idea,' I joked. 'He deals with a lot of noise complaints.'

'About time I fucking made one,' grumbled Eric.

He tended his garden almost to the point of feminine care, but inside you saw only the signs of a wearying bachelor life: an unwashed fry pan, the ash tray by the solitary armchair, bare walls. I wondered whether I wasn't seeing my father's life as it would have been without books and the law as companions, or without me to take care of.

Each year, Eric was seemingly more certain that he had a duty to guide me past my father's strange life, and closer to something like his own. He complained if he heard me coming home late from a party; I was wasting my youth. Or if I wasn't often enough at his place, visiting, consulting him about the vital business of the erosion of our crumbling dune, which like his temperament worsened with the passing years. He worried that one day I might even become a lawyer.

'That's what Dad wants,' I told him.

'Don't listen to him, you idiot. Do something you care about.'

'I'm quite interested in the law,' I said nervously.

'No you're not,' said Eric. 'No one is. What you're interested in is your own miserable patch. No lawyer but your father cares about anything else. And let's face it, he's a bit of a failure.'

It was meant as a compliment, I knew. 'I'm not going to work on boats, Eric.'

'That's exactly what you should do. It's in your blood.' It was just the two of us, but he seemed to draw me aside. 'I've got the apprenticeship forms. I'll get them.'

'Thanks,' I whispered.

He went inside and returned with the paperwork. 'You'd make a good boat builder, and a lousy lawyer.'

There was the Yorkshire bloodline. But otherwise I wasn't sure what quality Eric had located. Perhaps it was just that I was old enough to leave school now, if I wanted. Or that we liked each other and could spend hours talking about nothing in particular, apparently a central quality of boat builders, and also, I supposed, of painters sitting on the dune, and perhaps even of those who liked to write about these things.

The willingness to wait, until you knew where to wander to next.

Sometimes Claire would ring me at home and ask if Anthony was around. If he wasn't, we stayed talking on the phone, and the afternoon would pass while I sat on the hallway floor and listened to her voice.

'I wish Anthony was there,' she once said.

'Do you need to talk to him about something?'

'It's not that. But I like it when he's at your place. I wish you two spent even more time together. I wish the three of us did.'

'I see enough of him,' I joked.

There was a pause, and then she went on. 'Yesterday I was missing Anthony, but then I realised I wanted to see you and Anthony – both of you, together.'

'Well, I'm your friend, too,' I said.

'Yes, but you know what I mean.'

I wasn't sure I did, not completely. But one afternoon, instead of waiting for Anthony outside the school gates or riding home to talk to Eric, I found myself wandering across town towards Claire's school. St Margaret's watched over the coastline from the first step in the slow rise that took you out of town.

I was surprised to find that I wasn't alone: there were a few of us drifting up the hill, away from the shoreline and up towards a brick school chapel. We all took the same shortcuts across the second oval at the rugby league club, through the police car park, and then one of those private yards that over the years had become an easement, seemingly for state-school admirers of private-school girls.

I worried that there might be others going to visit Claire, but as we neared it was obvious they weren't there to meet anyone in particular. It was merely an assembly point. Girls in hockey gear poured out, and the boys hung back by the chapel, offering each other cigarettes. It began to rain lightly, and we leant against the chapel wall to catch what shelter we could from the narrow eaves above.

I kept an eye out for Claire, but, rather than wait any longer with the others, I circled the chapel hoping to find her on the other side. The boys were strangely courteous about this: they pretended not to notice me circling the building. Maybe I wasn't as odd as I felt, or being odd was part of what we were doing there.

I'd almost given up, and stood with the others on the front steps, when I heard Claire's voice. 'Where's Anthony?'

I turned to face her. 'I don't know. I haven't seen him.'

'What are you doing here?'

I didn't know what to say. 'I had some time. I'm meeting Dad in town.'

'Oh.'

'You're playing hockey?'

'Every Thursday,' she said.

We glanced towards a stone wall that protected the hockey pitch. Some of my own schoolmates jogged over there to join in a conversation with one of Claire's teachers. 'Will they have to leave?' I asked.

'If they call out.'

'Call out?'

'They think it's funny. "Good shot". "Great angles".'

I smiled. Actually, more than anything it sounded open. 'You should be grateful for the encouragement.'

'I don't care. They're not here to see me.' Her hair was tied back, but the rain worked free the strands at the front. 'I should go,' she said. 'I'm meant to be training.'

'Do you mind if I stay for a bit?'

'Yes.'

'You do mind?'

'You really want to hang out with those guys?'

I looked again at the wall. The teacher had left and was gathering the girls for a talk in the middle of the field. The boys seemed alright to me. Of course I wanted to hang out with them.

'Well, Dad's expecting me,' I lied.

'You'd better go, then.'

I walked back down the hill, and felt the light humiliation of being turned away. Couldn't we have pretended that I'd come up on a whim, and that I would watch her as idly as the others while she and her friends played hockey? Couldn't I be one of the spectators calling out bad double entendres, eventually sent on my way by a tolerant teacher and the rain?

An answer lay in my self-deceit. I wanted to see her on our own. And really that was all I wanted, nothing more. An hour when I could talk to her away from Anthony or her crowded life at the boarding school. A chance to listen to her properly, and to maybe discover if she loved Anthony in the way that I thought he loved her, or more in the way that I loved her.

In my mind, the main reason my father and Anthony got along so well was because they loved the women in their lives in the same way. They'd both come to read their love as they read books: something you could collapse into while also remaining fundamentally alone.

Sometimes Anthony copied quotes from poems and novels, especially from Dickinson, and the modern greats like Woolf, Lawrence and Waugh – writers we liked. He gave me his selection of quotes as keepsakes, and often accompanied them with his drawings – the first experiments of an artist who saw words as physical images. Often he read as a way of finding ideas for paintings, and he painted in order to cement his relationship with the shape of words, I thought, more so than with their meaning.

And then he began to illustrate the quotes with self-portraits. He emphasised to the point of ugliness his long neck, his broad and angular shoulders, his flat chest. But his handsomeness, his dissenting beauty, also appeared: the very finely drawn nose and his high cheekbones. He saw it, but as with his talk of Claire he also shaded his beauty into an idea. Something that could then be argued over, intellectualised, and even destroyed. And whenever I asked what Claire was like when they first met, he avoided the question altogether. Or he answered, 'Find out for yourself.'

I wasn't sure I wanted to try that again.

9

I was certain I'd learnt this: there was a great, poetical love that resided in thought, reflection and art. There was also an everyday love that was better captured by movement and sight and the brush of hands. And although beauty was the most unreliable guide, forever insisting on itself as final evidence of its worth, I sensed also that it formed a connection between different kinds of love. Beauty demanded something to happen: without it, it seemed you'd need the gravity of the moon, or the uneven sweep of the tides, in order to draw people out of themselves, and the two kinds of love onto the same section of the beach. Claire was *too* beautiful. All and everything this meant was that she made me want to understand both her and myself better – the two searches had become the same.

But I knew better than to make any more visits to the hockey field; I only saw Claire in Anthony's company after that failed trip at better discovering who she might be without him. And our visits to the beach, too, became less regular. They were fighting. Every few weeks, Anthony announced that Claire was leaving him. When I asked why, he said it was because he was an idiot, nothing more complicated than that. But this opened up quite a few possibilities. I knew that she didn't like it when he drank, or argued with strangers, or smoked marijuana and started talking about death and beauty as though, in fact, they were inseparable. As though they were the two ends of love.

He'd become very absent when he was stoned, and often this distance in him was a prelude to a physical disappearing. I wouldn't see him for days – he was either stuck at home or had escaped to other friends, people Claire and I didn't really know. It worried me as much as it did her. He'd find his way back. But until then, who knew where he'd been or what his father was like. He wouldn't tell me.

'You love her, don't you?' I asked him.

He replied by saying that was a stupid question, and of course he loved her. 'You know that.'

'Then why don't you treat her better? You should be around more, give her what she needs. It wouldn't take much to show her that you're trying.'

'We always end up yelling at each other.'

'Why? What do you fight about?'

'She doesn't want to love someone who's destroying themself.'

'Do you think you'd love Claire if she was like you?'

He answered that he'd never understood what Claire saw in him. 'I'm waiting for her to leave, but I'm not waiting forever.' It was a bleak joke, but true as well. Eventually, he said, he would have to push her away.

In a daily way, it was their painting that held them together: in a small town, it gave them a kind of innate support that only they could understand. But it also held the clue as to why they should keep trying. 'She sees you in your work, I know. I'm sure she does.'

'She hates my paintings.'

'But it's why she bothers with you. She'll never leave you. The two of you come together in the way you paint. Or the reason you paint. The way you find answers. You believe in each other.'

'She posed for me the other day. I keep repeating the pose she took. She doesn't really like it. She wants me to paint her as I see her: some kind of live painting, sketches, like hers. But this stance she had is so graceful. So perfect. She turned away, and was standing with her side showing towards me, with her arms above her head.'

'That's a classical pose,' I said. 'You're just painting her in a standard way.'

'Yes, I know. But it suits her.'

He brought out a roll of paintings to show me. I hadn't asked to see them. As he unfolded them, he criticised me for being indifferent.

'Just show me,' I said.

'You have to take some. Without asking. Isn't that the ultimate compliment – when someone steals one of your paintings?'

'Would it still be stealing if you've told me to do it?'

He unrolled his nudes of Claire, or rather his repetitions of a pose that he'd only once painted in her presence, but that had so captivated him since.

They weren't exactly studies of Claire, for, as with his self-portraits, he'd given her an unnatural angularity that stole some of her languidness, her ease with the day: her waist was narrower, her face paler. But the most striking features of her look remained: her thick black hair; a face that drew you down the sharp line of her cheekbones to almost girlish, thin lips; her slender arms. The startled, wondering expression in her eyes that asked not only *why this painting now*, but seemingly *why this person in my life*. Not even Anthony, searching for the symbolic, could take these from her.

I told him to turn away for a moment.

'What are you doing?' he asked.

'I'm stealing one of your paintings.'

While they were arguing, Anthony hung out with other girls – sometimes girls he'd met through me, and who were impressed by his antagonistic view of the school and the quiet life of the town. Despising sport and avoiding a suntan won you some credit with a certain kind – I suppose our female equivalents, and yet not the ones we could ever quite fall in love with, for they were too like us.

Sometimes, they gave me a chance as well. I wasn't hostile to sport, and in those days I was as brown as wet sand. But I did have the most important quality: a missing piece, and, crucially, one that could only be found by leaving Lion's Head.

Years on, I still had my scar from the accident. Somehow, when I talked to girls, it was present at the back of my mind. It didn't always inhibit me, but from time to time it stopped me going beyond the first encounters in the dark or at backyard parties, when the scar remained unseen. It made me self-conscious. Or perhaps I was held back because I was already waiting for Claire. As, in a way, Anthony was held back by the knowledge that they'd get back together. While he was with other girls, his paintings would continue to be of Claire rather than them. They hated him for it and left him.

Only once did I hear of Claire being with someone else. He was an apprentice mechanic, a local football star called Alex. After they'd been together for a week, he was ready to get married. We were shocked that she could be interested in someone so unlike us. We'd assumed that being awkward and ill-fitting was part of our appeal, but now we found out that wasn't it at all. I wondered whether there was a gap between what she liked about us and what we liked about ourselves. Maybe our difference was a drawback.

I scrutinised her paintings for clues of how she saw the world. Like Anthony, she wanted to draw the body, but unlike Anthony she was, at heart, a sensualist. She produced studies of our friends coming out of the water, or sitting in the shade next to the surf club. She only ever represented them in a realistic mode – and she was only ever interested in us in the same way, not as finished thoughts or ideas, but as indeterminate beings shaded in by light and movement. Her paintings were roughly drawn anatomy lessons, and they claimed that the body was symbolic enough. It didn't need further elaboration.

She very seldom read the books Anthony gave her. While she was with Alex, she returned them to me. It was after school. She also had drawings she'd done and that she said she wanted me to have. At first I thought she must have come for Anthony, that she was ready for a reconciliation with him. But she had with her a calico bag filled with his books.

'Could you give these to him?' she said as I approached her.

'He's still here at school somewhere. I saw him before.'

'It's alright. I don't want to see him. I'm sick of all his books lying around my room.'

'He won't take them,' I said.

'I don't care. You have them.'

'Sure.'

She could have left then, but instead she stepped a little closer and said she wished Anthony would stop reading altogether, and just paint and paint and paint. Paint forever, until he had it all worked out of him. That was where he'd find himself.

I didn't agree, not in those days. 'He doesn't want to find himself. Why do you think that?'

'He's the same as you. Your stupid fathers.'

'I miss you,' I said.

'Good luck with Anthony,' she replied.

I didn't tell him that Claire had been, or that I had his art books in my room. I didn't want him to think it was over.

Because Claire boarded, the three of us had seldom been together in the evenings. Anthony and I had once talked about trying to break her out. Now he missed her more and more, and was jealous of Alex. A little drunk on cheap wine one evening, he asked if we could make a night visit. It might bring her back.

The break-in was much easier than we'd expected. As it was a hot night, we managed to walk in through a back door that was kept open to bring the breeze into the dorms, and then climbed a wide staircase of wooden panels and hospital-white ceilings. Her room was called Little Annex; and, as if acting as conspirator, the school had placed the words in raised, golden letters on the first door at the top of the stairs. Our goal was impossible to miss.

She shared the annex with three others. They lay dead still and pretended not to notice Claire's escape until just before the door closed again. Then I caught their eyes opening, and I knew the whole thing would be all over both her school and ours before the end of the next day. It didn't matter. I handed Anthony the cask, and the three of us chased our own shadows across the hockey fields.

Claire complied until we got to the far walls. I guess she hadn't wanted to make a fuss when she saw us in the dorms. But suddenly she stopped, breathless, and tried to yell at Anthony, or perhaps at us both. 'What are you doing?'

I felt there wasn't a straightforward answer to that. I wanted them to be together, and I didn't know why. Or, I thought it might be because I was in love with them both, and in love with their togetherness.

Anthony wanted more wine. 'Come for a drink,' he said.

The thought of Alex seemed to flash in Claire's eyes, and maybe also the thought of how unfair she was being to him. 'Why did you come?' she asked, this time quietly. The sprinklers came on in the next field, thinning the sound of the crickets.

'It's the three of us,' he replied.

'No,' said Claire. 'I'm just along for the ride, aren't I?'

'It's the three of us,' I told her.

Again, Alex was present as a thought, and as a choice that might end the whole thing for good. She could have a proper partnership. And then she asked, 'Where are you going?'

We decided on a wall of stones and boulders that braced the first, wide bend in the river as it drew out of town. It counted as a local scenic spot: there was a wide gravel car park for those who wanted to stay in their cars. The last of these was leaving. When the car reversed and turned to face the road, its headlights scanned the river and then us. Anthony turned away, but Claire met the gaze of the lights with her own open stare. Her skin suddenly blanched white.

We sat on the rocks and began to drink. It was so intensely dark now that we couldn't see each other. You forgot where you were sitting until you spoke, and then the others appeared as well, outlined by replies in the darkness, a sonar system. It seemed the moment to chart something. For I knew this was the standing configuration now – the three of us listening for each other.

'What's going to happen to us?' I said.

'Don't ask questions like that.' It was Claire. Other times, she

65

would have waited for Anthony to speak. 'Enjoy this,' she said. 'It's so quiet down here.'

'I feel like it's slipping away,' said Anthony.

'What?' I asked.

'We're slipping away. I know we're all going to leave, but I often think about losing you.' I wasn't sure if he was talking to me or Claire, or to both of us. He went on, 'Don't you worry that we'll lose it all when school's over?'

'No,' said Claire. 'Can't we have each other forever?' Irritation in her voice, as though she and Anthony had had this conversation before.

'I'm sorry I brought it up,' I said.

Anthony asked, 'Can you see the river? My eyes are getting used to the dark.'

Yes, it was pulsing now, or that dank air that hovered over it and eventually stood in for a visible surface. A layer of heat came into view when my eyes adjusted, but disappeared when I looked again to the longer darkness of the sky.

'What's that?' I asked.

A car came down the driveway behind us, its lights off. I turned around as they switched them back on, and felt the last flicker of Anthony's shadow as it fell behind the rocks. Two police officers stepped out. They recognised me, the magistrate's son. 'You shouldn't be here this late,' said one, a younger officer called Gareth. 'Have you been drinking?'

'Yes.'

'Where are your drinks?'

'In the river,' I replied.

Gareth shone his torch, the light a yellow runway over a tarmac of water. Our box of red wine was drifting out, caught in a slow, circular current that was about to join the main channel. White plastic cups were tipped onto their sides, sinking.

'Is your friend in there as well?' Gareth said.

'I don't think so.'

'Hey! Come up.'

Anthony obeyed, and crawled up the rocks to the car park. He was embarrassed. I could see that Claire wanted to say something to him, but she didn't.

'Are you going home now?' the other policeman asked.

'Yes.'

'Do you want a lift?'

'No,' I said, 'we can walk. It's not far to go.'

I thought of asking Gareth not to tell anyone, but I didn't think anyone really needed to be told why Anthony had jumped, and what lay in store for him if his dad found out.

The next morning, the town heard about Claire's midnight escape from the dorm. It would have counted against some girls, but Claire was never judged in quite that way. Her failure, if there was one, was in thinking only of escape – of beginning her getaway early, and maybe with the wrong companions. With boys who were in their way more dangerous than the others, because we encouraged her to believe that she was a princess meant to break out of the castle, and not just the clever daughter of hard-working Greeks.

But it was different for Anthony. Two weeks later, my father received a visit in the night from the police.

'Is he alright?' I heard Dad say. I came out from the kitchen.

It was Gareth at the door. He wore the same expression as at the river that night – the opening of a confidence.

'What's happened?' I asked.

'Anthony's in hospital,' Dad replied. 'He's been beaten up.'

'Who did it?'

Gareth didn't answer.

Dad looked at me, and then gave Gareth instructions. 'Bring Anthony here when he's ready to leave. I want him brought here. He's not going back.'

10

My only meeting with Anthony's dad was so brief that in the seven or eight years since it has more or less disappeared, or has come to be folded into a dozen other meetings with families of friends. All I can say is that he was wearing a singlet, as in fact Anthony most often did when he painted – perhaps I am remembering Anthony. I would guess that he was shorter than Anthony; that, like his son, he had his hair cropped short, and that it had receded and must have begun to recede when he was young, at Anthony's age or only a little older.

Most acute is the memory of the thought I had: that I was in the company of the man who caused such fear for Anthony and his mother. At the end of the day, I knew him not as a person but as that effect. And, the effect he had on Anthony is where his presence in my memory is located still – in the awareness we had of Anthony's other life at home, and the escapes it led Anthony to attempt. Into drugs and sudden, new friendships he didn't share. Claire and I knew there was a life without us, but also that he would never show us.

Now, for the final weeks of his last year of school, I would get to help him, have him close. That was something good to have come out of the night of Claire's escape. I admitted to myself that a more troubling outcome was how often I saw Claire. For them, daily classes were more or less finished, and she came over nearly every day, sitting at the end of my bed just as she had four years before, when we'd first met at the hospital.

I began to dream about her. We met on the ocean floor. I didn't insist anymore that the whole world was joined down there, a place of meetings. I thought I'd left that philosophy behind with my younger self, left on the rocks after the accident. But my dreams were fixated on the possibility, said that I'd been right to hope for something there. In one that recurred, I walked into the dark, calm water. As I dived in, the ocean floor fell away into a labyrinth of black- and purple-walled caves. But now I wasn't sure that I was looking for my mother. It was a different feeling, one that caught me more in the stomach than in the chest.

There, in the water, I saw Claire. I heard her saying my name. Her voice came up from the bottom, released as a perfect song. She disappeared. Then appeared again, swimming ahead of me. I followed her. But she remained in the middle distance. All she'd say was my name. She smiled when she turned around, and kept turning around to check I was still following her. She waited for me to swim deeper, and then she went on, deeper and deeper into the caves, until I woke without her.

In the mornings, I watched Anthony paint. Mostly, he used acrylic paint and pen, very quickly drawing a dark outline for the figures that he filled in with smudges of black ink and only a small colour range – the main colour was blue, which he used for shading the way other artists used the varying heaviness of a pencil.

When he needed a break, he'd cook breakfast for us – always fried eggs and tomatoes. He was a vegetarian, and now that he was living with us he began a slow campaign to convert me. He never asked me to stop eating meat; only to eat whatever he was having, whatever he'd cooked. After breakfast, I went to school and left him to his painting or reading.

That November, after I was done with exams, my father asked me to travel with him on a work trip to Sydney. Soon after we'd left Lion's Head, I asked whether we could go to a second-hand book-shop while we were in the city.

'What book do you want?' he said. 'I might have it.'

'It's a book called *Markings*.'

'By Dag Hammarskjöld?'

'Yes.'

'But you've got that already. I've seen it on your desk.'

'That was Anthony's copy.'

Dad thought this over for a moment. Then asked, 'Do you ever suggest books for Anthony to read?'

'Yes. Well, your books.'

He smiled. 'Hammarskjöld died in a plane crash in 1961. He was the better kind of Christian, if you know what I mean.'

'No.'

'He wanted to understand people. He didn't have all the answers. That must have been refreshing in the fifties, when everyone had become so sure, and so frightened at the same time. He once said that if you wanted to know how things stood in a country, you spoke to women first. That was the best insight you could get. Not many religious people thought like that in those days.'

'I didn't know you were such an admirer of his.'

'Hammarskjöld was a good man, and it is a wonderful thing to read his thoughts in that book. But I'm not sure you should concentrate on great men. Listen to your own world, this world around you, before you spend too much time imagining another one. Life is on the ground around you.'

'You know, Auden translated *Markings*?' I knew Dad had read all of Auden. He trusted him as a poet, one not overly captivated by the moon.

'Perhaps it was because he was gay.'

'Auden was gay?'

'Yes, but I'm not talking about that. I'm talking about Dag, his sympathetic view of women. Sometimes gay men have a clearer sense of women.' After a pause, my father returned to my question. 'Auden had a fascination for all things northern. He and Hammarskjöld corresponded. But, yes, Auden thought Hammarskjöld was gay, like himself. I gather the translation wasn't popular in Sweden – they found it too free, too focused on Hammarskjöld's private suffering and loneliness. You heard people say that it cost Auden the Nobel Prize.'

'For saying that Hammarskjöld was gay?'

'For saying it, yes. Everyone thought it. But these things usually go unsaid.'

'Things are changing,' I said.

'You might think so,' he replied. 'But how well does Anthony cope?'

We were only gone for a week. We stayed at a modest hotel on Glebe Point Road. Dad worked every day at the university, while I spent the mornings reading and the afternoons walking near the harbour, mainly around The Rocks. I found art shops and a book exchange, and eventually my own copy of *Markings*, a hardback edition with a black-and-white cover photograph of a stone, seemingly modern but also very clearly inspired by the rune stones of Hammarskjöld's Sweden.

Reading his work, I couldn't find much evidence that Hammarskjöld was gay or otherwise, only that his busy public life as UN secretary-general hadn't relieved him of the harder task of filling in his nights. This, I thought, was less Anthony's problem than my father's.

When I got back to Lion's Head, Claire came to visit, and surprised me by saying that she'd missed me. My father and Anthony were talking about a book Anthony had read while we were away – *The Stranger* by Camus; a beach novel, Dad joked. Claire left them and asked me to join her on the veranda. What had I thought of Sydney? She said she couldn't wait to move there.

'It'll suit you, and Anthony, as well,' I replied. 'I bought some books and some oil pastels for him. Oh, and by the way, Dad told me he thought Anthony was gay.'

Claire seemed prepared for this. 'That's just a parent thing about boys,' she said. 'Parents always worry about male friendships. They don't think of girls' friendships that way.' She laughed to herself. 'We're allowed to be sensual with our friends.'

I hadn't realised that Anthony was sensual with me. Before I could think much of it, I asked, 'You don't think he's gay, then?'

'What do you think?'

My main thought was not about Anthony, but simply that it was getting harder to speak to Claire. It was hard to say anything without revealing everything, hard to match the direct way she examined me when we were alone. On the drive to Sydney, the conversation about Anthony had stopped, and in that moment I'd dismissed Dad's view of my friend. But in the days that followed our arrival there, in the afternoons that I spent walking by the harbour, I found myself returning to Dad's question, and introducing a new one. Who was Anthony in love with?

I looked at the shadowy green at the back of the dune. The sound of the ocean was ever-present, and I liked how voices sometimes got lost in it. They couldn't hear us inside. But if Claire and I stopped talking, I tried to catch the sound of Anthony and Dad together. I could just see them at the back of his office, standing at the bookshelf.

'I wonder why they get along so well?' Claire said.

'Dad loves a curious mind.'

'Is that why he avoids me? Am I not curious enough?'

'You're very self-contained, I'd say. It wouldn't ever occur to anyone like Dad to try to help you. He wants to help Anthony.'

I could have mentioned that she was just the type to frighten my father, even the type he would once have interrupted had he found her reading by the river.

I added, 'You have a happy father.'

'Yes,' she said, 'imagine a life with one of those! I get to worry about the two of you, instead.'

For my own part, I'd decided to follow Dad's advice and not Eric's. I would study law and become what Eric had predicted, a mediocre lawyer rather than a master boat builder, or, what I hoped I might manage even better, a writer. I knew that I wasn't bright enough for the law, and that I'd have to study hard to get in.

Claire, too. She said she was less sure of her painting than Anthony. She hadn't yet heard from the art college.

'Do you worry about his results?' I asked.

74

'No, the main thing is that he paints. He's not getting ready for anything. He's there already.'

'He showed me the pictures of you.'

She looked at me, I think to confirm my embarrassment, not because of any that existed on her part; to check that the discomfort was in my eyes as well as my voice. 'The nudes, you mean?'

'Yes.'

'I don't like them.' She was still staring at me.

'I'm sorry.'

'I don't mind you seeing them. Not at all. But his paintings of me are so hard – they're not even pictures of me. He's always saying women are more beautiful than men. "Women are the only beautiful objects for a painter." Then he paints me like I'm a man.'

'You don't look like a man in them.'

'He knows he's good. You know he's good.'

'Yes.'

'That's what his paintings are full of – his confidence.'

'You don't mean that.'

'When he paints me, he paints himself. That's why they're so hard. His pictures of me are brutal.'

I replied that this was just Anthony's way of meeting his subjects, of finding them. It could seem hard, but a better word was conflicted. He didn't know how to paint the surface alone.

To myself, I wondered how Anthony saw Claire, that is, other than in her role as the perfect subject, a perfect conflict in the matter of beauty. Better than anyone, he saw her beauty. But I still wasn't sure he understood that it demanded something back, and that he wasn't giving it to Claire. Beauty did not exist just so that you could gaze at it, but to ask you what you had to give in return. Claire was here, I thought – right now, she was fully here, and I wanted to tell

her that I was hers. She sat next to me still, and in her stillness was
such a current.

That summer, Anthony painted only her. He continued to exaggerate certain features – the angle of her elbows, the length of her
arms – as if to contradict the truth, which was that her silhouette,
her outline when she walked and moved, was always very even.
Instead, he brought her into the world of jagged edges, a truer world
if not a truer Claire. When I asked him about it, he said he was
spending too much time looking at books of Picasso's blue period.
  'Books that your father lent me,' he added.
  'Start learning about other artists, then,' I replied, 'maybe Degas.
Isn't he interested in women even when they aren't performing for
the artist?'
  'No man gets to have that view.'
  'But that's exactly what Claire wants to give you,' I insisted.
  'She can't.'
  I tried not to let the paintings change my own impressions of
her. Maybe it was too late. At some level, they were formative, like
memory moulds, and can now never altogether be separated from
those days, or how I first saw her body. Her pointed shoulder blades
and slim neck. Even her way of walking in front of me, my eyes
drawn across her shoulders and her middle back. Things Anthony
taught me to see. When she grew her hair longer, I followed its
reach as it wound unevenly around her neck and down her back.
  Anthony made my life harder by forever compiling an inventory
of her body, a reference list of visual memories that he shared and
analysed. He was obsessed with her collarbone. He said he spent
an hour tracing it with his finger, and then, after they'd made love,

he tried to draw it better than before. Or it was the fineness of her arms, or her nape, or that spot a little higher where the neck first begins to reach the ear.

What was that spot called, he asked me.

'I don't know.'

'When she puts her hands on my chest. She has small lateral muscles – she's not very strong. But when she pushes down on me you see her muscles there. I want to paint that muscle, but I want to paint it at just that moment. I want to stop her. It's so perfect.'

'Why are you telling me?' I said. 'Do you think Claire wants you to talk about it?'

'She knows I talk about us. Only to you.'

I wasn't so sure Claire knew that. But then, the next time the three of us were together, Anthony invited me to sit in on the sessions while he painted her, and Claire said she'd like it if I joined them.

She looked at me and added, 'You've seen a hundred paintings of me.'

But Claire wasn't a painting anymore. She was naked in front of me, posing. I tried to adopt Anthony's artistic view: she was a study, an example of a certain kind of beauty; perhaps of too much beauty, as well.

No: I decided she wasn't too beautiful.

My bedroom was small, and I sat on the bed, underneath my window. The view was out the side of the house, across the road as it curved in from the beach, to an unused field of low pine trees and the sandy clearings between them.

When I turned from the view, I saw Claire as she stood with her arms above her head, the same pose that pressed her ribs against the skin of her side and gave her pelvic bone the peculiar angularity that Anthony wanted. I said to myself that, if I'd painted her, I would have waited for the moments when she relaxed that pose and when her outline, the shape of her waist, was allowed to stand uncorrected by art or design.

It wasn't a bright room, either – the pine trees cast the light in spots. I tried not to sit in the shadows. But as the space dimmed further, it seemed my task was to study not only her but the light, too – to observe how a hidden source found its object.

Her body was a figure of the wind: when the pine trees moved, a different part of her was lit. The pulse of her stomach when she stood with her side to us; and, when the trees swayed again, the rim of softer skin on her lower back appeared.

For a brief moment, I wondered what I was doing there. How did I know that they wanted me?

Perhaps you can never be sure. But then after all we were here in my room; later, we'd walk along the beach and sit on my part of the dune, the section I'd once run over before I went swimming. There was something assuring in that. We listened to one another, and each knew how to wait in a way that allowed the others to say what was on their minds. In those longer moments, I knew we were three together, not two and one.

Over the slow final weeks, it seemed we focused entirely on promises that we made to each other about the future. We needed them before the future could begin, because they gave us a way of saying goodbye. Maybe that's what the paintings were: preparations for the days when we'd want to remember each other in a very particular light, the light as passed through the pines of Lion's Head.

Claire said Anthony was going to stay with her at the farm for two weeks before they moved south, and asked whether I would come, too. In front of Anthony, she added, 'I'm not sure I want him for that long on his own.'

'What's going to happen in Sydney, then?' I said. 'Won't you be stuck with each other all the time there?'

'Oh, Sydney's full of things,' she answered. 'And we'll house-share with some other people. He won't get to annoy me.'

My role when I joined them in Sydney would be to keep them sane. Further on, I would fund their art. It seemed so obvious that one day I'd be a lawyer with money, and equally obvious that any money that Anthony or Claire earned would always be spent the day they got it, on art supplies, books or music – but in Anthony's case I suppose also on the temptations of the other world he joined when we weren't meant to be watching.

He didn't exactly hide it from us that he was using harder drugs now, but without being asked he withdrew himself from our company whenever he wanted to get high, coming back in the morning when he was sober. We didn't get to meet his suppliers or his companions, but he wouldn't have denied they were there.

When I told Claire that I wished he'd stay in on those nights, or at least let us in on this second life, she replied that he couldn't. 'He thinks you're strict,' she said, 'or more high-minded than he is. He'd be embarrassed if you saw that he was hooked.'

'We could try to stop him.'

Her anger, then: 'What do you think I'm doing every day?'

In the mornings, if he'd been out all night, he'd tap on my window, and when I opened it I told him to use the door. But he'd insist on coming in through the window. 'I don't want to wake your dad.'

'You already have.'

'Not properly. I don't want to wake him properly. If I come through the door he'll think there's a visitor.'

'But you are a visitor.'

I made coffee for us, and we pretended that we hadn't woken my father. After that, it would be impossible to get Anthony to bed. He would still be lightly high, and wanted most to talk about Sydney. I understood it, and that sitting talking to me was the easiest way to watch the clock winding down.

He knew that he could be hard work. But I didn't mind; in fact I craved his company when he wasn't there. He overcompensated for his strong views on pet topics by complimenting me on everything I did. He said he loved the poetry that I'd begun to write; he would use my poems in his next paintings. He said that I was getting more handsome. He corrected himself, elaborated: 'But you're small-town handsome. You're good-looking, nice-looking, but not properly handsome. Really handsome men are more striking than you are.'

Like so many of our conversations, this one was a little ridiculous. It was alright that he'd come home in the morning, woken me up. He didn't need to tell me these things. I asked him whether he wanted more coffee. But he had a way of going on. He said, 'The other day, Claire asked me, "Isn't Ted very handsome?" Don't you think it's strange that she's asked me that? What would you do if your girlfriend told you how handsome somebody else was?'

'I'd have a better idea if I had a girlfriend.'

'She's got a crush on you. You know I don't mind, don't you? I don't love her any less for it. I'm not angry. I was thinking about it:

the two of you would be wonderful together. I can actually see it. There's something I love about the thought of you together. I told her that. Maybe she's talked about it?'

'Of course not.'

'I told her you'd make a good lover. A caring lover. I told her that I could imagine you together. Isn't it funny: the thought of it makes me happy.'

'You're full of shit sometimes,' I said, 'especially when you've been out all night. You're making this up as you go along.'

He was indignant but not put off. 'I'm not making it up. I've thought a lot about it.'

'One of your theories. I don't see the point of talking about it.'

But he had to have the last word. 'It wouldn't hurt me if you did it. It would be beautiful.'

11

Claire's parents had left Greece after the war. Like my father, before they left they hadn't properly thought through what it would mean to live so far from Europe. The farm they'd bought in Australia was a hundred kilometres inland. But visiting it was like going back to their home in Karoussades, the village in northern Corfu where they were brought up. They'd arrived and planted olive trees and tomato vines, which they still harvested for the Saturday markets, and they grew their own grapes to make watery lunch wine.

Two weeks before Christmas, we met Claire outside her school gates, and then Nikolas appeared in a white delivery van to take us all out to their farm. During the drive, Anthony and I took it in turns to sit in the back on empty wooden crates, beside coils of rolled-up netting. Nikolas was rather quiet, but he'd brought cold drinks and bread, and every time we passed a shop or a service station he asked whether we wanted him to stop to buy us more food.

'I think we're fine,' I said.

'I have cheese as well,' he said, and as he drove he reached across Claire to a paper parcel in the console. I picked it up for him. 'Yes!' he called out. 'Open it for you boys. Claire doesn't eat!' And then we laughed, as though all was solved.

Claire put her hand on his forearm and replied in Greek.

'What did you say?' I asked.

'I told him that you two don't ever work hard enough to get hungry.'

She was right, but during the two weeks that followed I discovered how pleasurable it could be to rest the mind and use the body, to work hard. As, to our surprise, did Anthony. He suspended his views about local farm practices and agricultural imperialism, and with me woke each morning dazed by a bodily weariness that neither of us had experienced before.

At first light every day, a ute appeared outside the farmhouse and Nikolas honked, and then the two of us sat in the back for a slow half-hour's drive into the fields. On the way, we sang loudly and badly. Over the bumps, Anthony claimed a hidden talent for trilling. It sounded like a warble. But I taught him parts of 'O sole mio', and it became our song for the mornings. The sun was our sun.

Most days, Claire stayed at the house. But she spent her time outside, too, and I tracked with almost religious care how her shoulders and arms browned. Very quickly, she changed from the private-school girl back to the daughter of her migrant parents. Her heritage also revealed a source of her trust in the body, the 'permanent temporary' as Eric called it. She spoke Greek more than English, prepared long trays of lamb and salad, and took over her father's work on the home garden.

'It turns out you're a peasant,' I said, watching her prepare a meal.

'Is that a surprise?'

'I thought you were a princess.'

'I suppose I was brought up to be both,' she replied. 'That's the Greek way, isn't it? Greek girls are peasants and princesses.'

The kitchen was time-stamped with the family's first wave of prosperity, in the early eighties: the brown cupboards placed evenly along a wall of pale orange tiles; shallow double sinks; plastic appliances dulled by use. It was the decade of our births, too, but Claire moved around the kitchen a little uneasily, as someone who'd been away as much as she'd been at home.

I'd seen that Nikolas respected her enough not to be too possessive; he didn't seem to protest that she was home with two boys. But as I stood with her in the kitchen I asked, 'What would your dad think of Anthony's paintings?'

She didn't want to answer: even Claire kept some parts of her life separate. Eventually she said, 'Your dad isn't the only thinker in the world, you know. Mine doesn't spend hours alone in the study. But he understands me; he knows why I paint.'

'Don't be angry,' I said, even though I liked it.

'What would your dad say if you didn't become a lawyer? I know you want to write.'

'You don't need to convince me. Parents don't know us that well.'

'But do you really know? Sometimes I think you don't see it. You don't see what you've chosen.'

'I know my future's got something to do with him.'

'That's odd, isn't it? You shouldn't need a law degree to feel closer to your dad.'

'No,' I conceded.

'Change your mind, then,' Claire said. 'You might find something better.'

It was good advice, but for the time being I was satisfied with another task – with weaving the mysteries of my father, in this way, into those of Claire and Anthony, until he became a background stitch. Whatever Dad wanted for me would do.

*

Christina, Claire's mother, would stand behind me at the dinner table and stroke my hair, which I'd begun to grow long. 'Hair as soft as a girl's,' she would say.

As a joke, Claire adopted her mother's habit, and also that of touching my forearm when she spoke to me, just as she and her mother did to Nikolas. Once, when I was crossing the highway with Anthony and Claire, and we had to run to make it across, Claire reached for my hand to hold. Was it in preference to Anthony's, or was I just the closer one? But Anthony stopped and watched us.

Claire's parents loved him – I hadn't expected that, and nor, I think, had Claire. But he was so easy and lovely that fortnight. And he was at his most handsome that summer, especially after, as if in keeping with our song, he let himself take some sun. He was brown, he'd been spending time outside with me and Claire, and he'd proven to be the best worker.

He allowed himself to be cast as the Adonis among us; and, to Claire's extended family of Greek migrants, who came for Sunday lunch at the end of our first week, gathering around a long table of plastic serving bowls and carafes of light wine, he was like the sun.

If there was a counterbalance, it came in the afternoons after work. From the farmhouse we rode on horseback along a riverside track down to a swimming hole that lay some five kilometres away. I rode behind Anthony and Claire, who touched hands across the track. Claire wore a long skirt, which she folded into her lap as she rode. The hem of the skirt swung to a summer rhythm.

When we arrived, I sat on the bank while Claire and Anthony stripped and ran into the brown shallows under a swinging rope.

'Why don't you get in?' Claire called.

'I have a horrible scar,' I said, trying to be light. 'I'll frighten you and that man next to you.'

'Leave your shirt on, then, monster,' she replied, laughing.

I didn't answer. I stayed on the bank and watched them keep a polite distance from each other. This was some kind of courtesy to me, a sign that I could still get in if I wanted. Sitting there I wondered, as I had when Claire posed naked for Anthony, how they could stand to have me along like this. Surely they'd have preferred me to leave them in peace.

And yet I also understood that there was something about having me there that made it easier for them to get along – to be satisfied in the moment, the sun and the water and the late feeling in the air, each as the perfect companion for the others. If there was something between us that couldn't be said, those afternoons it went happily unspoken. It could wait.

I got up and pretended to look for a platypus that lived further along the creek. And then I came back, sat and watched them talking in the water. I sensed that they were talking about me. My response was to continue a nervous habit that I still hadn't dropped. I traced the scar with my index finger, and wished it would dull. And wished I didn't find excuses to stay out of the water.

12

By the time we got back from the farm, my aunt Lillie had arrived in Lion's Head. Dad had told me she'd be visiting, and I'd come to expect a dark-haired relative with my father's rocky, Yorkshire bearing; that particularly Northern way of displaying self-possession.

She had none of that, though; she was still the woman I'd once misremembered as my mother. Her hair, now grey, was wavy and blew across her face as she spoke. She was constantly fighting with the wind to keep it in place, and her other habits were somehow part of this struggle with her hair – as though at any moment the whole of her might become scattered. It kept her hands busy, and she moved her face from side to side in order to shift the weight of it.

She was older than my father – I suppose in her early fifties when she came to visit us – and yet she bore the air of someone much younger. You had the feeling that coming into middle age had been a relief for her. If there was one thing in which she was settled and in no sense scattered, it was her singleness; Dad said it had always been that way, since she was a girl, and that you knew even then that she wouldn't ever marry. Growing older had allowed her to meet that destiny still more happily.

Then again, her attitude to herself was a happy one anyway; it was like the happiness that I saw in the photograph of my mother – direct and unhurried. Lillie knew how to laugh at herself. She told me she'd come to visit us in Australia because she wanted to see the birds. And then she laughed at herself for saying such a thing to me. 'I'm very fond of birds, but no expert,' she added ceremoniously. 'They are God's creatures. And our most loyal companions. Yet most of the time people don't even think to notice them.'

'You believe in God?' I asked.

'Yes, of course I believe in God.'

'I thought our family wasn't religious. Dad said it was more Mum's side. He makes a point of it, actually. He says he prefers to find God in the things people do, rather than in the idea of God.'

'He doesn't mean it,' she answered, a little sternly. 'But, yes, your mother was brought up that way – she had a more conservative upbringing, I suppose. Much more so than me and your father. But she thought about religion in her own way, too. And maybe I was more from your mother's side of the family, anyway. At least that's how I felt when I met her. I felt like I'd finally met the real side of my own family.'

'You were close?'

'Oh, we were the best of friends.'

'You lost her, too.'

'Yes. We have that in common.'

'You and Dad?'

'The three of us.'

But Lillie and my father were spending very little time together. He never took holidays, and, even now when we had a rare visitor, he held to a regime of retreating to his study in the evenings. It fell to Anthony and me to be Lillie's guides, to turn on the fan in her room and make sure the mosquito coil was lit on the back balcony outside it. And mid-mornings, Lillie drove my father's car while we gave directions, as often as not to Nambucca, where we spent our time searching for the right place for a cup of tea.

'Would you like to see the rocks?' I said. 'We can walk to the heads from here.'

'Oh, I can see rocks any time.' I wondered what could be so special about Australian tea, but she added, 'You, on the other hand …'

So we took our seats in one of those over-quaint cafés in among the shops, rather than along the sea front. She could wait until the afternoon to go for her walk for the day. Anthony told Lillie about his paintings, and that he and Claire were leaving for Sydney soon.

'I expect you'll miss one another,' said Lillie.

'Not a bit,' I replied, watching him. 'Anthony's the most difficult person in Lion's Head. There'll be a whole week of celebrations when he leaves.'

Anthony had something better to say. 'What Ted means is that he'll miss Claire the most.'

'She's lovely,' said Lillie. She looked at me and then at Anthony, and I think for a moment didn't quite know what to say next.

We ordered a late breakfast of scones. A wave of light rain blew past the awnings. 'Don't you want to see more of Dad?' I asked. 'I wish he'd take a holiday so he could join us.'

She considered the idea, one neither of us thought realistic, and answered, 'Well, I feel like I have him here. You are your father thirty years ago.'

'Are we that alike?'

She pushed her hair aside, to examine me more closely. 'Your mother's there, too. You've some of her mannerisms, her way of watching the world. And qualities, too. You're rather serious, Ted, aren't you? As she was. I see it when you're reading. You read as though you need interrupting.'

'Dad once said the same thing about her.'

'Yes, I know the story. I was wondering whether he'd told you.'

I could tell that Anthony didn't want to interrupt, but all the same I suddenly felt exposed in front of him. I said to Lillie, 'Still, I wish Dad was around for your visit.'

'Don't. There's no one in the world I understand as well as your father. And your mother. We spent a lot of time together, even after they married and came back from Durham. I was there when you were born. Your dad hasn't changed a bit since then. I don't mind that, I expected it.'

'I thought he was more open to people once.'

'Then you saw an unusual side of him. Your father has always expressed himself in silence.'

'But he talks so much about the voice. I know more about Haydn than I know about my mother.'

'No one knows their parents,' confided Lillie.

'I want to know them.'

'Then one day you'll have to come to Whitby to find out for yourself.' Lillie seemed to grow angry with me. 'There's only so much I can tell you, Ted. Come for yourself. You'll see everything. Bring your dad with you. He needs to come home, even if it's just for a day. An afternoon in Whitby would change a lot.'

*

That afternoon, while Anthony stayed at the house, I joined Lillie for a walk along the beach, and also, by the end of the day, in mimicking her favourite local birdcalls. She and I made Eric wonder by trying to bring the birds to the front steps of the house. I was still surprised that we could have so close a relative who was open to the world. Where was my father's introspection?

But under it all was a similar kind of prompting, rather like my father's. She shared his desire, and Claire's, to guide me past my closed world of rumination, past that habit of my parents. My father had voiced this desire in lessons about opera and in his insistence on the material world of legal rights, while Lillie, certain that my father wouldn't ever open the family file for me, eventually left me with a note that ended with this: *Birds migrate. That's a miracle. There are all kinds of mysteries. All in the hands of God but also in how we listen to them, and follow them home.*

I folded the note and began my own family folder, one to match Dad's drawer. For now, it consisted of letters from Anthony and Lillie that had been slid between the Dickinson anthology and my journals, which themselves were mainly poems about Claire, but also about windows, smoke, and the warm salt in the evening air.

My father would drive Lillie to Sydney to catch her flight. And he told her he would go to Whitby if she ever needed him. But otherwise there was no hurry to go back to England.

He said he'd spend a few nights in town. By the time he returned, Anthony and Claire would be down there in Sydney, too, on his heels. As he left, he hugged Anthony and asked him to pass on his best to Claire. He said he was sure they'd succeed at art college. They were meant for that life.

13

Low trees climbed up the squat rocks of the Head, and down its back to the water's edge. At the end of the day, dust blurred the low sweep of earth and rock that shaped the isthmus to the other side of the cliff. But behind us, an orange projector flickered through the leaves, and the sea was lit like a screen.

Anthony sat with his arms around his knees.

'Is there anything you want to talk about?' I said.

'Not really.' He handed me a cigarette. 'I've never asked you: does your dad know you smoke?'

'Yes.' He'd known for about a year, I thought. 'He says he doesn't want me to smoke cigars, though, like he does. He thinks he smokes too many.'

'Do you? Smoke cigars, I mean.' When Anthony didn't get an answer, he said, 'Mine would kill me. There you go. No, hang on. He'd kill me if he found out, even though I think he knows.'

'That's no secret. Everyone knows your dad wants to kill you.' It was meant as a joke. But it was too dark, even for then. 'Don't ever come back,' I told him. 'That's the main thing, isn't it? If you're going to go, go for good, right?'

'Yes.' But he had something he wanted to know, a final something before he and Claire left. That's why we were still sitting at the beach while she was up at the house. He asked, 'Will it be hard for you when Claire's gone?' And, as quickly, he checked himself. 'You don't have to answer that.'

I wasn't sure what to tell him. Perhaps it would be a mistake to tell him anything at all. But Anthony wanted it said, and that evening seemed to be the moment to share it – probably the last chance before they left. Not share, no. Rather, say openly aloud.

After a pause, he said, 'I can't believe we're going. I have that feeling that it might all be a fantasy.'

'Yes. That's just because it's close. It'll feel real when you're on the train. Then you'll know it's the best thing you've ever done.'

'You're not as impatient to leave, though.'

I turned towards the house. 'Not in the same way,' I conceded. 'You'll get to start again. And that's why you're going. You can paint, and no one's there to tell you that you shouldn't.'

'Will you go to Sydney?'

'Yes.'

'And it'll be the three of us again.'

'I'll come down and make sure you're looking after Claire.' I wondered whether we could stop there. 'Should we go up?'

'You have to tell me,' he said, 'if there's something on your mind.'

'There's always something on my mind. It doesn't mean much.'

'Truth is better than kindness.'

'That *sounds* alright, even if it's completely wrong.' But with that I finally gave him what he wanted. I stood up and took a step back, towards the house, and told Anthony that I was in love with Claire.

'I'm sorry,' I said. 'I don't think she knows. She's too much in love with you to notice.'

I wasn't sure I agreed with myself on this, but Anthony undid the apology before even I could. 'She notices everything,' he replied warmly. He wasn't ready to get up, and I hovered behind him. 'That's who she is,' he said without turning around. 'Isn't that what you love about her?'

I supposed it was.

'She doesn't make it obvious,' Anthony said, and finally stood up. He brushed the sand off his legs. 'She's not going to tell you she knows you're in love.'

'Have you talked to her about this?'

'No.'

There was a stillness between us, a spot of darkness in which I wanted to add that Claire had noticed for the simple reason that there was a part of her that needed to notice me.

Wanted to notice me.

I thought that underneath it he was angry. But he laughed and hugged me, and gave me a kiss on the cheek. I never much liked these kisses of Anthony's, and even less so at that moment. I wasn't sure, as he was, about testing the gentle and decorous ways of Lion's Head. And by all the rules, now wasn't the time of day for Anthony to kiss me on the beach. This was our chance to have a fight, and for him to leave in anger. To accuse Claire of disloyalty and vow never to speak to me again.

But that wasn't Anthony, and I loved him almost as much as I loved Claire. I loved how he liked the possibility of disapproval, including mine. And how he pressed always for more. 'We should kiss on the lips,' he said, 'like they do in Scandinavia.'

'Men don't kiss on the lips in Scandinavia! Where do you get this rubbish?'

'Lighten up, Ted,' he said. But he wouldn't let go of me, not yet. 'Isn't it funny? Or strange?' he added, almost to himself. 'But

I'm completely happy for you. I'm happy that you, serious Ted, are finally in love.'

'Fuck off,' I answered.

He laughed, as if relieved that I was annoyed with him and the stupid things he said. He continued, 'Did you have to fall in love with Claire?'

'I guess so.' He let go of my arm. 'It'll calm down while you're away,' I said.

As we turned up to the house, we seemed to decide that we could leave it at that: there was a chance that things would settle down. I'm not sure either of us believed it. I hadn't seen much in my life to suggest that matters of the heart were calmed by time. I needed only to look up from the beach to my father's study to find how little some people aimed for change.

Nevertheless, that was the hope that Anthony and I left between us in the air that evening. It circled us like cigar smoke until it was caught by the breeze and carried up to the house, where that night we would have my father's study to ourselves, just me and Anthony and Claire gazing at the dune from his window. Yes, that's how we left it. Anthony and I were both in love with Claire. And what was unsaid, what stood between the lines we'd managed or remembered, was this feeling: surely love was strong enough to bear it.

14

A few weeks after Anthony and Claire left for Sydney, Dad asked if I wanted to join him on the morning walks that he took along the beach. He'd offered in the past, but this time it felt more like a suggestion – something he thought I needed.

We left at six, and walked for an hour until we reached the Nambucca estuary and could see across the water to the rock wall on the other side. For most of the way, Dad set a fast pace; it wasn't easy to talk very much. When we stopped, we spoke mainly about school. He was worried about my marks, and whether I'd make it into law.

'I was the same at your age,' he told me, 'a bit up and down. But my dad helped me. He taught himself most of what he knew, but he liked science. He understood it without really having to try very hard.'

Dad said he wished he could do the same for me now, but he thought I would be better served by extra classes after school. In March, he rang around for a tutor, and found Clive, a local who'd just returned from his doctoral studies in Melbourne. He taught high-school kids in one of the study rooms at the library.

One of the others there, Brigit, had also come for help with maths and physics. She was in grade twelve at Claire's school, and told me she'd seen me hanging out with Claire and Anthony.

'You must think about them a lot,' she said. 'Are they doing okay in Sydney?'

They seemed always to be in my thoughts. I could have told Brigit exactly how many days were left until I'd be following them to Sydney. 'I'm in a friendly year,' I said instead. 'And there's so much happening at the moment. We don't get much time to think, do we?'

On the eve of their departure, Claire had told me straight that she wouldn't email. She didn't like writing much, and anyway she didn't see the point. She left predicting that when we met again things would be as natural as ever. That we didn't need to write for that to happen.

Anthony didn't share Claire's confidence, and insisted that I write every week, and that we keep in touch by letters. He thought you could say more that way, that email was inferior. In my letters to him, I wrote about my studies, and the solitary nights I spent working towards the better marks I needed to get into law. Sometimes I sent him the poems I wrote. I mentioned that Lillie hadn't been in touch again, and that the idea of Whitby had fallen quiet, as suddenly as the birdcalls changed and started later each morning. I had the feeling that things hadn't ended all that well between her and Dad.

The long letters that I received from Anthony in reply were filled with discoveries, most often of the mind. Anthony had fallen into radical feminism, and MacKinnon was quoted at length. Then double consciousness, and Eco, and the Russian masters, and Peter Singer, and from there to Coetzee's *Waiting for the Barbarians*.

I followed him into these illuminated corners of the shadowed mind, a mind I didn't really get to see in its own terms. I was worried that he was covering up the fact that the move wasn't working out. And all this reading seemed to have little impact on Anthony's obsession with Claire's beauty, which through the letters still manifested most intensely as artistic admiration. This now seemed to worry him. She was too good for him, he wrote. I wondered why, and asked him to explain what was happening. He wouldn't answer. He said her hair was longer than it had ever been; she wore it down her back. It was a black flame. Everyone at college was obsessed with it.

When, without telling him first, she cut her hair very short, Anthony took this to mean more than it did – that she'd finally tired of him. She was telling him it was over by taking away one of the things he'd come to love most about her. They would break up soon, he declared. Then, by the time I wrote back to say he was over-analysing her, and that he'd once loved her hair shorter, he'd already forgotten his preference for long hair and said he'd never seen her face properly until now.

I knew from watching my father that if you filled the days with enough activities you could confine reflection to those few hours that remained at night. I'd made it onto sports teams and the school committee, and I spent many afternoons in a group organising social nights, fundraisers and school events, or at training and the after-class group at the library.

Soon it would be Anzac Day, when I'd be reading out a poem to the school assembly. 'I'm nervous,' I told Brigit as we waited to start our lesson. 'The local MP's coming.'

'She'll love you,' replied Brigit. 'What poem did you choose?'

'It's a Dylan song. It works read out rather than sung.'

'We love Dylan at my place. Mum puts him on every second night.'

Clive arrived, and we settled down to our work. Brigit sat across the room from me, at a table that faced mine. She had the habit of sitting cross-legged, and bundling her skirt into her lap. At the front, her blond hair was knotted into braids.

Often, Clive blocked the view to her desk – he liked to stand between our desks. But once I looked up from my book to see that Brigit was watching me. For a moment, I thought she wanted to say something, but as quickly she turned away, as though I'd been the one who was meant to speak.

Afterwards, as we left the library, I asked her about school and then about her brother Joel, whom I'd met a few times.

'I'm going home to study,' she said.

'Haven't you done enough for today?'

'Mum's expecting me.'

Brigit seemed to be inspecting me again, and this time I tried to meet her gaze with a less blank expression. 'You can come and have dinner with us, if you want,' she said eventually.

Brigit and Joel lived with their mum, who was from Holland. She'd moved to Australia to be with Brigit's dad, but he'd left a few years before and now lived in Brisbane. He'd married again and had young kids with his new wife.

'We all get along,' Brigit told me as we walked to her house. 'Even Mum loves Jenny and the girls. We alternate Christmases at their place and ours.'

I liked theirs very much: compared to our house, everything seemed so fresh. In the living room a low couch and beanbags sat in front of a slim, wooden bookshelf lined with framed pictures and a collection of painted plates.

'What does your mum do?' I asked.

'She's a psychologist.'

I must have looked surprised, for Brigit added, 'Don't worry. She doesn't try to work out people she knows. Or my friends.'

After I met her, I couldn't imagine Brigit's mum interfering in anyone's life, not even her daughter's. She told me to call her Tess, and then cooked pasta, offered us a glass of wine, and said she'd be going out to a committee meeting. Did we know where Joel was?

'I think he's still at the park skating,' said Brigit.

'Well, there's a plate of pasta for him when he wants it.'

When Joel came in an hour later, he called out hello from the kitchen and Brigit called back about the pasta.

'Too easy,' he replied, and a moment later we heard his bedroom door close.

'He won't come out again.'

'What's he doing?' I asked.

'I don't know. What do fifteen-year-old boys do in their room at night?'

'Their homework,' I joked. 'Or write poems about girls.'

I left Brigit's place at eleven, and then remembered I hadn't told Dad that I'd be in late. I found him sitting in the study, reading and seemingly unconcerned.

'I know her mother,' he said when I told him where I'd been. 'She helps out at the court now and then.'

I waited for more, perhaps a flicker of interest in Brigit's mum. Nothing. But after I said goodnight, I looked for something similar in the evening I'd had with Brigit. Wouldn't that be good, if we could switch our attention to those who were close by?

In the months that followed, I often ate at Brigit's place after class. We helped each other with maths and physics questions, and in between we sometimes exchanged short family biographies. She told me about how much she loved her little half-sisters in Brisbane, about Joel's obsessions with skating and surfing, about her mum's inability to stop working all the time.

In return, I gave Brigit the story of my mother's death, if not in the way I'd once explained it to Claire. I didn't say that I felt Mum was with us here in Lion's Head, or that I'd once tried to meet her in the water, in swimming out to meet her in the deep. But I told Brigit that one day I hoped to travel to England to visit Mum's grave, and see where I'd been born.

'Hasn't your dad wanted to go back before?'

'I don't really know. We've never talked about it. We don't talk about Mum very often.'

'Do you think you should? I guess not all families are like that. Talking about everything, I mean. Sometimes I wish Mum didn't want to talk over everything. I think she loves it when we hit a new *issue*.'

'What will she say about this?' I asked.

'This?'

'Yes, about me coming over after class all the time.'

Brigit hesitated. 'Oh, I don't know. Maybe something about not forgetting the basics.'

I waited for her to explain, but I had to ask. 'What are the basics?'

She feigned a serious tone, maybe her mother's: 'Don't do all the chasing.'

*

101

The next day, during our morning walk, I raised with Dad the idea of us going to Whitby one day.

'Yes,' he replied, stopping for a moment. 'Lillie would love to see you again.'

That would be fine, I thought. 'And we could visit Mum.'

'Yes.'

'Is it a nice place, where she's buried?'

'I suppose so. There are some pretty gardens there. And the sea, of course.'

'Don't you miss Yorkshire?'

'I miss some things. Walks, a bit like we're taking now. When I was young I used to walk or run everywhere. I especially liked the mornings – after it stopped raining in the night and the wind dropped. The sea was still. You could smell the seaweed and the fish. I miss things like that. It's very pretty.'

'It sounds like a nice place for Mum to be.'

'She loved it. The coast was her natural home. When she moved there from Durham she said she felt like she'd come back. She would have adored Lion's Head.'

I was going to ask about their first years in Whitby, and about Mum's swimming. Before I could, though, Dad began walking again. A little later, when we stopped at our turnaround point at the beginning of the estuary, he asked about Anthony. 'Did he get a chance to talk to his mother before he left?'

'Yes,' I replied. 'She helped him to pack.'

'And his father?'

'He avoided him.'

Dad thought for a moment. 'Well, he's clear of that man now.'

I hoped so. Anthony had so seldom talked about his father that it was hard to tell what the final impact would be. 'I don't always know

102

what's going on with Anthony,' I said, 'just that he needed to get away.'

When we got home, Dad asked whether he could read one of my poems. I'd never talked to him about my writing, but perhaps Anthony had.

'I've written one about our walks,' I said.

He smiled. 'Will you read it to me?'

'I don't want to read it out.'

'Leave me a copy, then.'

'I'll copy it out neat,' I said. But I did better than that – I typed it up later that day and left a printed copy on his desk.

Walking with Dad

We walk too fast to speak.
Whatever could be said
is left silently between our steps instead.
We have the same rhythm,
Dad and I.
When we rest, me puffing,
watching the sea,
he's telling me what to read.
The Road to Wigan Pier,
if you want to go north.
Dad rests his hand on my back,
almost says more,
but we've stopped long enough.

When it was time to nominate our choices for university, Brigit said she was going to put down Brisbane as her first choice. She wanted to be close to her dad. She'd be able to live with him, and help out with the girls.

'What about you?' she said.

'I'm sure Brisbane's great.'

'But?'

'It feels like a long way away, for some reason.'

'It's the same distance from here as Sydney. We're halfway between.'

'I guess we are.'

The next week, Brigit didn't ask me to dinner. She was as nice as before, helpful with my maths problems. But it seemed also that she'd decided something about me, something that couldn't be changed. I replaced her missing invitation to dinner with my own. 'Dad's not too bad in the kitchen,' I told her.

'I should study,' she said. 'And so should you if you want to get into Sydney law.'

15

I told Dad that it was simple. I wanted to go to university in Sydney because that's where Anthony and Claire were. He asked whether I wouldn't be happier in Brisbane, in a new place – Brigit would be there, and I could make new friends. It seemed that however much he liked Anthony, my father feared his influence. He was still firmly the Yorkshire man, and he expected effort to yield results. He didn't want me to return from Sydney with four undergraduate years spent studying Anthony's relationship with the world. For him, that was a greater concern than the one that had formed in my mind: that I'd waste them waiting for Claire.

Here and there in Anthony's letters an actual fact about their lives in Sydney had slipped through reflections and crises, and over the months I was able to assemble the following. They'd found a place, a share-house that was leased by a law student from Denmark. Both Claire and Anthony loved art college, but Anthony was arguing with the lecturing staff; he'd threatened to leave, but had been persuaded back by the course coordinator. Sydney was expensive, sometimes they didn't eat. But it was everything they'd hoped for: a proper city, a kind of artwork in its own way, reaching towards the even greater cities. Now and then, Claire visited her parents at the farm. The bus took her directly inland; it didn't stop at Lion's Head on the way. But Anthony was sure he was never coming back. They went to parties: Claire was doing well, but she didn't much like the art world.

So I left Lion's Head feeling I knew very little, and unsure of what to expect. When Dad finally delivered me to my college on a grey January day, I all but forced him back into the car, rushing him to say goodbye so that I could phone Anthony.

He told me they lived close by – their share-house was on Glebe Point Road, where Dad and I had stayed on his work trip. I followed Anthony's directions through Victoria Park, along the green and hemmed-in base of the university grounds, and crossed over to Glebe. I had a dim awareness of all the things that I wasn't stopping to see, things that would usually have halted me, especially as they were to be mine, my home: the bookshops; the cafés; the posters that fought for space on doorways; the mess of ground-floor apartments with their doors open, hallways cluttered with books, bicycles and unmatched furniture.

I was too anxious and excited to stop.

On the phone, Anthony had said they were all at home. But for a brief moment, I didn't think it was Claire. A girl standing in a light dress against the pale wall of a house, a girl so obviously at home here that it seemed to be someone else. She didn't look herself, but part of the city. I only really knew that it *was* her when she saw me and ran over, a silver fish in the shallows. She jumped up and held me.

It was the beginning of a glorious day. Anthony seemed much better than I'd feared. He'd lost weight, and wore loose clothes, I thought to cover just how thin he was. But he was so overjoyed to see me, held me for a long time and kissed me on the forehead;

his excitement persuaded me that the restlessness and flickering darkness of his letters were more a matter of rhetoric and flourish than experience. In those first moments, seeing him buoyant and Claire so at ease, absorbed by Sydney, I was sure that everything was alright and that moving had, after all, been the only thing for them to do. Theirs was a true escape, then; his father could finally be allowed to fall behind him.

The house was much older and nicer than I'd expected. It perfected that old-fashioned quality Claire and Anthony always had – located them in the same warm tones that occupied Claire's paintings. That was why it was a home: they had found a painting to become part of. Worn, ash-grey timber floors ran the length of the house. The front windows were narrow and high. As the sun found some space under the clouds, the front room became a small chapel; the floors could equally have been of stone.

'Where's your housemate?' I asked.

'He'll be home soon,' said Claire.

'You'll like him,' Anthony told me. 'You're very similar. A bit quiet. He likes to be the clever one in the room. Like you.'

'You're giving me a hard time already,' I said.

There was colour in Claire's cheeks. She smiled at me and said, 'Have you missed us?'

'Yes. You know that.'

'I've been so nervous.'

'It's just me,' I said.

They didn't have much furniture, but what they did have was lovely: a reading chair, shelves across the living-room wall. 'How did you afford all this?' I asked. 'Did the place come furnished?'

'Our rich housemate,' said Claire.

'He bought all this for you?'

'He bought it for himself.'

'You won't want to spend much time at college,' said Anthony. 'Don't become one of those law students who devotes a life to that.'

'Is there another kind? I'm going to go to lectures, if that's what you mean.'

'The different kind is the kind that stays with us. Ted, you're home now.'

Anthony wanted to bring out his new paintings while it was still light, and just us, before Jens got back. He presented his latest works as a great change. It was true, something was changing – the subjects had expanded. He'd begun to paint animals, and they expressed a playful side, one that in the past he'd kept out of his work. There were memory pieces of the ladies doing tai chi at the Rotary park. And landscape studies drawn from our fortnight on Claire's farm, companions to drawings she'd made at the same time.

Yet I found myself agreeing with something Claire had once said about his work: he painted himself, even in the landscapes. Maybe all artists were like that, or maybe he needed to. In painting, he had somewhere to put himself.

Claire was still nervous.

'Relax, it's only me,' I said again.

'It's just that I want you to like what we've got here. We waited so long to come here. You're the only one who can really see how we're doing.'

I thought her nervousness might also have something to do with Jens not being there yet. He was part of their new life, and of course she wanted me to like him. She said Anthony was wrong. Jens and I were not at all alike. We were both law students, that's all.

*

108

He arrived with bottles of wine. 'You are Ted! At last!' I was going to shake his hand but he pulled me to him with his free hand. 'I have wine!'

He put it down on the kitchen counter and laid out glasses. Claire watched me, waited. Those things she knew I'd notice: his looks – 'properly handsome', as Anthony might have said – and his dress. His hair, shoulder-length and fair. A beard trimmed short, in places more red than blond. A young man, but older than us in his ease, and more complete in his appearance. That's the photograph of that day, taken with the timer: the four of us standing at the bench, toasting Sydney while Claire laughs, finally relaxing again.

We began to drink. Jens rested his wine glass against his lips. 'My lips got burnt today,' he said, when he noticed me watching him. 'I'm learning to play cricket. You should join our team.'

'Thanks,' I said.

There was only the faintest Danish accent. It was overlaid with a London intonation, the English of an exchange student.

'You should wear sunscreen,' said Claire, 'with your skin.'

'You didn't play cricket in England?' I asked.

'We were there for a couple of years only. Now my father has just been posted in New Zealand.'

'You didn't want to go with him?'

'No,' Jens said. 'I wanted to come here.'

He turned to Anthony and Claire, as though to say it had been a good decision. 'C'mon, Ted,' he said, 'let's drink.' He seemed to speak in toasts. He tapped the bench and added, 'I've got something else for later.' He laughed, and I joined in, even if I was still a little jealous of how assured and permanent it all seemed, the familiarity of their new life to them. But it was alright, surely. Anthony began cooking while Jens and I drank too quickly. Jens looked over his glass at me, and I tried to seem at ease.

Anthony announced that we were going to celebrate our reunion with his Tibetan cooking. It came out as a stew that could have been produced in support of any of his causes: vegetarianism, pesticide-free farming, localism; civil rights in Tibet, Nepal, Bangladesh.

'It's very good,' said Jens. 'You are the lentil king in this house. No doubt about it.'

'Do you like it?' Anthony asked me.

'I should,' I said. 'I do feel morally improved.'

'Is it the meat that's missing?' said Jens, grinning.

'Yes. And the flavour.'

Claire and Anthony laughed, and Jens reached for his glass. 'Are you a cook, Ted?'

'No. We've always agreed that I'll pay the bills. So that's why I get to be rude about Anthony's food.'

Jens leant forward. 'I don't need to protect Anthony. You've known each other for years, right?'

'Five or six,' I said. 'He knows I love him for more than his curries.'

'Maybe that's lucky,' said Jens. 'I'm sorry, Anthony, but he's right. It doesn't taste of anything. Was that your idea for the dish?'

'Oh, fuck you all,' said Anthony, and picked up our plates. 'Shut up or I'll make you eat more.'

And that was how the night went, by turns a little awkward and lovely, warm. After dinner, Jens pulled out a small plastic bag of black hash. He sprinkled it into a long cigarette that he rolled one-handed. 'Something I learnt from a Scotsman in Shepherd's Bush,' he said, giggling.

'Really?'

'No, of course not, Ted.'

Again, I was laughing with the others. Anthony put his arms around my neck and kissed me. I was drinking much too quickly. Then the hash took hold. I leant forward in my chair and stared at the floor. 'The wood,' I said. 'What wood it is.'

'Is it moving?' asked Jens.

'No. It's the grain. It's such a grey grain. How did it get so weathered? Did it rain? We're inside!'

'It's the type of wood,' said Claire. 'It's an old-fashioned wood. That's the way it goes.'

'They had different wood in the old days?' asked Jens.

'Of course they did,' said Anthony. 'The whole world was different in the old days.'

'I have to go to the toilet,' I said. But when I got there, I stopped at the sink and looked in the mirror. I checked to see whether I was turning grey, along with the floorboards.

Claire woke me with coffee and the sight of her legs under one of Anthony's long shirts. She noticed me staring at the soft turn of her inside leg. 'You've seen it before, right?' she asked, smiling.

Not quite. I'd seen the blue period, not the Degas. She pushed me along the couch and sat down. Her hair still smelt of hash and Anthony's awful cooking.

'Do you want me to put some music on?' she said.

'Not yet. It's too early.'

'How's your dad?'

'I don't know.'

She put her hand through my hair and said, 'Ted the swimmer.'

'Once,' I said.

I finally asked about Anthony, and how thin he was. She turned the question on herself. 'I don't know why we look so terrible. We don't eat enough.'

She lit us cigarettes. I asked, 'Have you stopped eating meat?'

'I suppose. But I only ever ate meat when I was on the farm. It doesn't make any difference to me. Maybe you can talk to him. Tell him to take better care of himself. He gets so pissed off when I bring it up.'

'Does he use anything stronger than hash?'

'They're all on acid.'

'Him more than the others?'

'He drifts off. You know him.'

I said I'd talk to him. She stood up. 'Go back to sleep,' she said without turning around, still a little stoned.

But by the end of my first week in Sydney, I was used to Anthony's appearance. It was another version to be added to the many others that met and played off each other in his self-portraits, and then somehow migrated into the world of his everyday. The debt to the blue period had been folded into a Gothic collage of medieval scenes. In them, he existed as several characters, each blended or obscured by their relation to another. Sometimes his faces were painted over each other; it was hard to tell which he preferred, which one was meant to invite the sympathetic gaze. What mattered most was the confusion.

'You won't ever resemble your father,' I said to him. 'Even the most accurate self-portrait doesn't look like him.' We were in his room, and I sat on the bed while he rolled his paintings out in front of me.

'That's not what worries me.'

'What is it then?'

'That it's too late. It's too late to come out of it.'

'Come out of what?'

'Well, you're right. Him. But not how he was. I hate what he left me with. Grime.'

'That isn't you,' I said. 'That's a memory of the life you had. You're out of that now.'

'I'm such a coward. I've turned into it.' He stepped over to a bundle of pictures in the corner of the room.

'I don't see it.'

'That's because you're Ted. You're like your father.'

'I wish you wouldn't compliment me. You're avoiding the issue. Listen to at least a bit of what I'm saying. You're out of it now. You made it to Sydney, to this. I can't believe you got such a good place. It even comes with its own Dane.'

He brought out new studies of Claire, ones he hadn't shown me on my first night in Sydney. 'Do you like these?' he asked.

They were gentle portraits, melancholy but also like Claire's drawings in how they presented fragments rather than whole ideas. They were genuine studies. 'I like your work,' I told him, 'but I always look for happiness in them.'

'Take some of them, please. I don't like having them around all the time. Decorate your room.'

I said I didn't want them – I didn't have anywhere to put them – but he gave me a roll all the same. 'You have to visit me,' he insisted. 'I missed you last year. Now that you're here, I realise I've been waiting all year for you to arrive. We're addicted to you, Ted.'

'Then do me a favour, too, and take better care of yourself.'

'I'm fine,' he answered. 'Everything will be fine. It's the three of us again.'

I walked the pictures up to the Mitchell Library, read at a desk, and then carried them with me through the open, stone corridors of the university – back to college, where I unrolled the paintings and tried to find one to put on my wall. The best candidate was a portrait of Claire sitting, fully dressed on a high-backed wooden chair. It wasn't quite a stately pose, but holding it up against the wall gave me the feeling of having arrived at court. I didn't want it above my bed. I rolled the pictures back up, and left the wall blank.

16

In my first year away from Lion's Head, Anthony eased my entry
into a group that wasn't quite mine to join. He wanted me, or
perhaps himself, to feel I'd arrived in Sydney at the same time
as him, and a backfilling exercise began. Most of his new friends
were in the various departments of art college: painters, sculp-
tors, photographers and jewellers, filmmakers – it was as though
Anthony had chosen one friend from each form. For his sake, they
offered me a place as observer, and eventually, I think, liked me as
their privately sponsored non-artist – one to keep at hand, in case.

I didn't tell them that I wrote, or that I had artistic hopes of my
own. Saying that would have been like telling them I was in love
with Claire. No, I was in Sydney to study law and to be with my
friends. I joined them at their shows around town, and normally
ended up at the after-parties. And although I was quieter than most
others there, I gradually discovered I was the type you could talk
to at the end of the night, when things settled down and there were
reasons to stop yelling.

Most of the exhibitions were held in a gallery above a Thai
restaurant in Newtown. You climbed a narrow, wooden staircase
of trapped spice smells that were gradually replaced by those of

budget wine and cigarette smoke from the other direction. At the top were small rooms with walls pock-marked by the dents of past exhibitions.

I wasn't always sure what to make of the paintings and installations I found. The aim was to shock; that was obvious even to me. But beyond that, it was merely identity politics doing its best to confiscate art. At one show, I turned from a collection of close-up portraits of vaginas and tried to tell Jens that I didn't find the works very appealing.

Jens replied that the trick was to stare for as long as it took for the vagina to disappear.

'What do you find in its place?' I asked him.

'Deep space,' he replied. 'I am looking past the pubic hair and into the origins of the universe.' I liked his response; it made me laugh. 'At least Anthony doesn't paint close-ups,' said Jens.

In the next room, a black-and-white film played. It repeated a scene in which a cut was made with a razor blade into the side of a torso, just above the ribs.

'What do you think of it?' he asked.

'It makes me sick. I really don't understand it.'

'There's some erotic charge there, don't you think?'

'Would you find it an erotic experience to be cut like that? Or do you want to do the cutting?'

'Don't be so serious, Ted. I know about your accident; Claire told me. She said you wouldn't like this room.'

'I don't.'

'Let's go then. If you don't like something, you can leave.'

Jens led the way out, and we crossed town to Rose Bay, to the home of a gallery owner who liked to be surrounded by students. Apparently, he was chasing Anthony. His walls were covered in nudes, the type that oversimplified the body into a few strokes of ink. Hundreds of art books were collected on scaffolding trestles. Outside, on the deck, the floors were lined with Persian rugs. He said he'd bought them in Shiraz.

For most of the night, I sat beside a swimming pool with a girl whose boyfriend was inside talking to Anthony, both high on acid and as far away from each other as they seemed from us. I could hear their laughter, but I hadn't spoken to either Anthony or Claire since we left the gallery.

The girl sitting next to me said she always liked to be the one who got to choose the music at parties. It played on outside speakers concealed in the corners of the patio roof. I thought of my father, and how he might like some of it – she'd put on Elvis Costello. Her name was Beatrice.

'Like Dante's?' I said.

'Maybe. What does that mean?'

'It would mean you're out of reach,' I replied.

She wanted to tell me she wasn't like her boyfriend; this fact seemed urgent. She didn't like acid, and only ever listened to new music. She said she liked music more than grass – it did more for her. I told her that I liked the smell of grass; I thought it was a bit like the smell of cigars.

A thin film of smoke crossed the surface of the pool. Beatrice took off her dress and slipped into the water. She was naked, and as she swam backstroke towards the edge, she lifted her waist to the surface. I saw a small island of pubic hair and wondered whether I ought to find the origins of the universe.

'Come in with me,' she said.

'But your boyfriend?'

'He's in another world. He doesn't care.'

I stayed out of the pool, but shifted to the edge of a step. I was wearing shorts, and felt the water reach up to my knees.

'Come in,' she said again. 'I'm waiting.'

'I can't swim.'

'I know you live at the beach.'

'I can't swim,' I repeated.

Beatrice dived under.

'Strange boy,' she said when she came up again, and swam to the step. She lifted herself out of the water. Her shoulders were high and pinched. Then she put her hands on my knees. 'Come into the water, friend,' and she pressed herself against my chest, kissed me. She pushed again. The small of my back was against the edge of the pool.

'You're strong,' I told her.

'What do we do now?'

'You feel very lovely.'

My shirt was wet. A light shone from under the eaves, revealing my scar through the cotton. 'Go inside to your boyfriend,' I said. 'He needs you.'

'I don't care about him. He's selfish. He only comes for drugs. Get in with me. I want you to fuck me.'

'No.'

Beatrice put her hand over the scar. 'It's sexy.'

'No. Your boyfriend's inside.'

Beatrice slipped away and stepped out of the pool, stood behind me, dripping. For a moment, I thought she was going to push me in. But she put her dress back on. She said, 'Claire will never love you the way she loves Anthony.'

I watched her walk away. She held her arms out, a snow angel, and against the deck lights a silhouette: her hips and waist were to

118

be held, but not by me. I wanted her, but I didn't call her back. She was still dripping as she stepped inside, and jumped into the living room and shook her hair. I heard the others laughing as she pulled the screen door closed.

I stayed outside for a minute before following her in. When people began to fall asleep, I made coffee and took a couple of sips, and then I walked back across town to college. I preferred these long walks home to sleeping at a stranger's house. I wanted to be downtown in that hour before dawn, during the last untidiness of the night, and during the slow exchange of night workers and the first morning commuters. I walked myself sober and out of the atmosphere of those groups.

Anthony hated me leaving on my own. But often he disappeared as well, and by mid-morning Claire would be phoning me to find out where we'd gone at the end of the night, and where he might have ended up.

I seldom had an answer. I told her that he'd be back, and that I'd call as soon as I knew where he was. Overtired, I'd amble back down towards the Cross in case he was there, asleep in the open. And then to Darling Harbour. But who knew why he left like this? Now and again he just signed out, needed to get away from us as much as he'd needed to get away from Lion's Head. Those mornings, the ones I spent chasing his shadow, made me want to go back.

17

The soul selects her own society. If I was possessive of Anthony and Claire, I also knew that in Sydney we would each have to find other friends and other paths to pursue. In the years that followed, they sometimes drifted out of view, and then back in – wasn't that why we'd come? The city was meant to give us chaos, not the familiar. And if not entirely chaos, then at least the exhibitions, the house in Glebe Point Road and Jens's good-natured, Danish sarcasm; the drug dealers at the Cross, the serious girls at college who wanted Claire to move in with them and get away from Anthony. There were times as well when those things were too much for me, and I stayed away.

What I hadn't expected was that chaos, proper chaos, wasn't in Sydney but in fact still lay in Lion's Head, with those things that my father and I had watched over, in ourselves, and in those nights when he listened for Mum in opera and I swam. In the city, the distractions actually formed stillness, and then it seemed that there could be no greater chaos than the waters of home.

I missed Dad, and during the first years of my degree I replaced my correspondence with Anthony with what became almost-weekly letters home. I told him about Mr Green's impossible lectures on taxation law, and he wrote back with advice on how to survive not only Mr Green but also taxation law and long lectures, what notes to keep, how to rote learn. *Find the main question*, he said. *That's the only way you remember.*

In my replies, I confessed to him that I wasn't a good student. I struggled to remember case names, and then I'd panic over which ones I'd cite in the exams, a panic that stopped me relating to the material in any real sense. I didn't follow his advice; I didn't connect what I was learning to the questions that the law wanted to answer, and that quite possibly I wanted to answer as well – I never found out if I was interested or not. Instead, I stayed up all night writing about my friends, and then rewriting summaries of lectures, hoping that some of it would eventually be seared inside, one understanding alongside the other.

There were exceptions, moments when I joined the brighter students and felt connected to the course. I learnt that I was a good speaker; in my third year, I managed a top mark in legal theory; and, that same year, I felt for the first time properly at home in a law subject – in international law. It was a subject that took me back to conversations that my father and I had once had, and I liked our lecturer, an Englishman – the one with whom Dad had been co-writing reports.

In the mornings, you'd see Dr Andrews walking hurriedly through Glebe on his way to the university. He was thought to be a little mad, having moved to Australia after he'd formed the notion that he was on an IRA hit list. The imagined threat of a car bomb normally stopped him from driving to work. On the rare occasion he did bring his car, he checked under it with mirrors before leaving for home.

During the exams one term, he stopped us to ask whose bag

was ticking. I hadn't heard the noise, but now that he pointed it out, it was there – an alarm clock left in a bag, perhaps. No one came forward, and Dr Andrews declared melodramatically that he now had no choice but to dispose of the bag. He rushed it into the middle of the lawn outside and called security. We watched from a silent examination hall while he waved his arms, demanding it be destroyed. It was obvious that the guards were more worried about him than the bag.

I wrote to my father about the incident, and told him that no one had ever claimed the bag. My father replied that Dr Andrews was an unusual man, but his behaviour was entirely justified: Andrews had written articles about the IRA, and came to Australia as an exile. Dad ended by saying that I should remember him to my lecturer, and he hoped he'd be in Sydney soon.

When I called in on Dr Andrews at his office, he said, 'I should have realised who you were, with your surname. Your father married the girl of our year.'

'You were at Durham together?'

'More or less. He was at Durham and I was at the pub.'

'That sounds better.'

'She passed away, didn't she – your mother?'

'Yes, before Dad and I came out to Australia.'

'Well, you have your father's knack for argument. You can tell him that.'

'Only in this subject,' I admitted. 'I haven't done well in the others.'

Dr Andrews took me on from there, and it seemed might help me to some extent understand the law. Survive these next two years, he said, and I'd be free to think again.

*

When my father next came to town, we met outside Dr Andrews's office and caught a taxi down to the Opera House. For an evening, we were returned to those nights we'd spent together in Lion's Head, to a meal by the water and then a concert of Bellini, Donizetti, Strauss and Verdi. He asked after Anthony, and I told him that we were seeing less of each other.

'Is that because of his drug use?' he said.

'I don't know.'

'Is he painting?'

'Yes, they're both very good.' They would soon be having their graduating exhibition. 'Anthony's work is selling, but Claire doesn't show hers very often.'

'I wouldn't let go of them, if I were you,' said Dad.

It was a brief exchange, but that advice changed the nature of my next letter home. I began to excerpt a suite of thoughts about Claire that hadn't stopped since I'd arrived in Sydney – things I could never have said to him in person, or indeed have said to Claire.

Dad,

You told me once about how you and Mum met, the story about going up to her on the bench. When you were talking, I got the feeling that you'd already decided to marry her, or that you hoped to marry her, before you talked to her, if she'd have you of course. You interrupted her on the bench because you knew you'd eventually propose to her. I see now that the same thing has happened to me, but in my case it was Claire who sat down next to me, interrupted me. After the accident, when I was in hospital, Claire sat next to me and I feel that the two of us decided on that day that we'd marry. You must agree that's possible, that we can see the whole cycle of some events the very moment they begin.

But I'm not sure whether that's what was going through Claire's mind, or ever has struck her in the way that it struck me.

I'm completely bound to Anthony, and I won't give my feelings away to Claire, even if she knows anyway. He isn't jealous, and I could kick him for that. I want him to be jealous. I would be. He shows me that I would be a terrible husband, possessive and demanding – not at all like Anthony. Their relationship gets worse and so I find myself keeping some distance. I want them to work it out, and I can only get in the way. Is that right, Dad? Should I let them be?

I love her, and I wonder whether you still love Mum as much. Does it last that long? You don't have to answer, I know you don't want to talk about it. But with this time away from home, I find myself thinking that I will drift out of the world in that way you have, and one day end up on my own in Lion's Head. That's how it goes, right?

I love you, Dad.

He replied that same week, but he didn't answer my questions. He said he'd be in town one of these days, and we'd talk better then. He had something to give me: the picture of my mother that, he wrote, he should have given me years before.

18

I did as I'd promised in my letter home, and needed to do for myself – I gave Anthony more time alone with Claire. For months at a time we wouldn't see each other, and then, as though to even the ledger, we met even more regularly than before. It felt as though our years in Sydney were to be structured by the two extremes.

On the days we got together, he was as hard to flee as he'd been when he came in through my window on early mornings in Lion's Head. Once in a while, Claire would join us for an hour. She wanted to know how I was doing in my studies, whether I would stick it out. And she would ask after Dad. But usually it was just Anthony and me, and once I'd skipped one class I was ready to skip them all.

Each time, he asked if I'd met anyone. When I said that I was still single he told me to relax, to read less, get myself off campus and spend more time with him and Claire and their friends. He was hardly the one to tell me to think more about people than work. His life concerned only painting; the various battles he fought in the everyday world were merely the final signatures he gave to his brushstrokes, the life markers of his style. He fought with the teaching staff – about the canvases he wasted, the cost of paints, studio time, access to the best models. And Claire, as well, was still part of his work, which was too much a part of him. I told him that was why they fought so much. He ignored my criticisms and said, 'You might as well be getting sex, even if you're too serious and well-read to have a relationship. Our friends sleep with anyone.'

I answered that they smelt of art materials and incense; it was off-putting. He retorted, 'You smell of books. You spend too much time in the library. You know too much about the law. You're even getting a bit dusty, like your father. Like your friend Andrews.'

It wasn't true. I was still a very ordinary student. When I wasn't in class, I wasn't in the library, but more often wandered around Newtown and Glebe instead. I caught the ferry to Mosman and then climbed the streets of hillside homes to Bradley's Head Road and down the other side to Balmoral Beach. It was the sort of beach where you could sit in shorts and a T-shirt and read without anyone thinking you were odd, unlike Bondi, which was closer but seemed to demand the baring of flesh.

Anthony came if there were going to be rocks and cliffs to climb, as we'd had growing up. He liked the shapes and shadows of headlands; despite himself, that was part of what he loved about Sydney, too. We'd walk and walk, and he'd swear about cars and traffic and the abrasiveness of life. And then, over the course of an afternoon, the anger settled and we were back to talking about Lion's Head, art books, and records that he wanted to give me. Half the books in my college room were his.

I was never angry – that, he said, was why we were so different and why he loved me so much. No, I replied. Anger wasn't a character trait, as he seemed to paint it. Anger was an emotion. And, anyway, didn't he realise how often I was angry with him? I hated it as much as Claire when he went missing, and when Claire had to collect me to go looking for him. I said, of course the world was abrasive if you picked arguments with drug dealers and art dealers and then slept at their houses.

Maybe he wanted more of my stern, self-important rebukes, for a week later he took a job waiting tables at a strip club in the Cross. The girls were sure he was gay and adopted him into a circle that was concerned only with hair colour, tans and a collection of beauty techniques – all of which Anthony related to me as essential education and context for all the literary heroines I fell for and might one day write. He loved the girls as much as I loved Emma Bovary, and brought them to parties where, they told me, they felt more false than they did in the clubs.

While I listened to them one evening, and watched their crossed legs, I glanced across to Anthony. I was more and more worried about his appearance, which only ever got worse. When the girls left for a better party, he yelled about the awful businessmen who lunched at the strip club. While he gesticulated, he bumped one arm against a side table.

'Why do you keep working there?' I said.

'I need the money.'

'There's other things to do. Why don't you sell your body? Or run drugs.'

'How do you know I don't?'

'Or you could teach painting to housewives. They'd love you. All that angst wouldn't bother them. They'd find it charming. You could return to your tai chi roots. Ladies by the waterfront.'

'I'd rather model for them,' he said. 'I think there's something morbid about teaching. Or, about me teaching. I taught myself; I don't know anything about technique. I still don't.'

I looked at his arm. The spot where he'd hit it was already swollen and blue. 'Your body's a mess.'

'Actually, the opposite. I don't have any of the shit in my body that you put into yours.'

'And I don't bruise when I bump into a coffee table.'

'You're much fatter. You should walk more.'

'I should move in and clean you up.'

He stopped me, stood up and kissed me on both cheeks. 'We need more to drink.' He added, 'Anyway, I wanted to tell you something. Claire wants her own place. She wants to move in with some girlfriends. It's her way of breaking up.'

'Sit down.'

'I've got to go. We need booze.'

He stood waiting for me to release him. I said, 'She just wants you to clean up. It's not easy to watch you doing this to yourself.'

'I don't blame her at all.'

'You're defeating yourself if you let her go. Then you'd be right about everything.'

'I'm black all the way through.'

'Don't talk rubbish.'

'I am.'

'Do you want to leave? Go for a walk?'

'I don't know.' He apologised for drawing attention to us, and sat down. 'I'm just scared, Ted. That's all it is. I get these awful dreams.'

'What dreams?'

'I go to the doctors and I ask them over and over to examine me and all they'll tell me is that it's black fluid inside. I tell them that there must be something else there. I say I can't be made only of black fluid. I get so angry about it. So they look again, but they can't find anything.'

'Claire sees something. That's why you have to keep her close. Don't let her move out.'

'She should be with someone else, someone like you. You're in love with her. It's such a good thought.'

'I hate it when you say that. Be jealous, for Christ's sake.'

He faced me. 'You're all kindness, Ted. It's the nicest thing I can say to you. Claire said it, too, by the way. It's always been so obvious that you're in love with her.' He stood up again. 'We're all hypocrites, Ted.'

'I don't want any more to drink,' I told him.

'Yes, you do.'

Anthony wouldn't stop her. He wouldn't try. Instead, they fought for another two months about how he wasn't stopping her, until it was too late. Claire moved out to a share-house on the other side of the campus, in Newtown. I heard it first from her. I was on the bus when she phoned, wanting to give me her new number and address. She said this time it was final.

'Are you going to be okay?' I said.

'What does that matter?'

'It matters to me that you're going to be okay.'

'I don't know.'

'What about Anthony? Can he stay where he is?'

'Jens is around until the end of the year. He's going to pay my share of the rent.'

The bus was crowded. I hated having this conversation in public, but I didn't want her to know that there were others there. It made me quieter; I must have seemed distant. 'I'm going to leave you alone for a while, aren't I?' I said.

'Maybe that's best. I don't know.'

'Normally when people aren't sure, it means they want to be left alone.'

'Normally that's it.'

At last, I decided to tell her it was hard to talk now – there were too many people around – and we hung up. I got back to college, and took the staircase to my room. I promised myself that I would leave her be. I'd concentrate on my exams. Eventually, I'd take any job my father thought would suit me; I would live on the North Shore and I'd walk to work in the mornings and catch the ferry home in the afternoons.

Why? Because Claire would always be in love with Anthony.

Jens and I had begun law in different years, but he travelled through the course slowly – he seemed in no hurry to return to Denmark – and so we were often in the same lectures. After them, with brains softened by subsections and case law, we drank together at the student bar. With Claire gone and Anthony at the house or missing somewhere, Jens and I tried too hard to be convivial, and rushed when we spoke. But we couldn't find topics we liked to talk about together. We drank too quickly instead, and as best we could avoided talking about absent friends.

He suggested time and again that I should do some further studies in Copenhagen, after I'd finished my degree. 'They're taught in English. And then afterwards you could go into diplomacy,' Jens said. 'It's just the life for you.'

I didn't have the marks for that world. But instead of saying that, I replied, 'I don't know. It's just my father and me. We don't have any other family, except an aunt in England. It'd be hard to be away all the time.'

'But your dad never visits. What difference would it make?'

'He's been. He and Dr Andrews go to dinner. It's a late romance.'

'You even spend your summers here,' Jens pressed.

'Yes.'

'Don't you miss the beach?'

'I live in Sydney. In a way, it's the same as living in Lion's Head – Sydney's so close to the sea.'

'Copenhagen is on the sea. You'd feel at home there, too. You could live at my parents' house, if you wanted. They've got plenty of space. No one's ever there. You'd have the place to yourself.'

I had no interest in going to Denmark, but there was no way of convincing Jens. I got the feeling he'd decided I needed saving. 'Where's your mother?' I asked. 'She isn't in New Zealand with your father?'

'She won't leave Denmark, not that far, anyway. Dad says they live at a convenient distance.' Jens smiled. 'He's a cold bastard.'

'Like you?' I tried to joke. It fell flat. At last, we gave up on Denmark, and changed the subject.

'Have you seen Claire?' he asked.

'No.'

'She's your friend, too. Not just Anthony.'

'Yes, she's my friend, but she needs time. I can understand that. We were so close, as a group.'

'Is that what she said?'

'No, not exactly.'

Jens glanced over to a group of girls who'd slid in along the bench next to ours. Without turning back to me, he said, 'It's you, isn't it?'

'What do you mean?'

'You're the one who's staying away.' He got up and said hello to the girls. 'You're law students, aren't you?'

'Yes,' said one.

He pointed to me, and they arched their backs. 'That's Ted.' Then Jens added a line that only he could manage: 'He's very serious. I've been trying to lighten him up for a while, but now I need to get some drinks.'

'Why are you so serious?' a girl I knew asked. Her name was Olivia.

'I'm not.'

We joined their table. At the end of the night I slept with Olivia, and woke up wondering if I really had. That's how it felt when I was with someone, a waking sense of improbability at how time ticked along and brought new people in. She spoke about a time we'd met in the past, at a party. I pretended to remember, and then apologised, 'I forgot.'

'I know,' she said.

It was very early in the morning. I was still drunk. The light in her bedroom was divided along a border of blue dawn and street-lights. I asked if I could leave; I wanted to walk home. I crossed over to Glebe Point Road, hoping to find a café open and then hoping to find Anthony home. But Jens answered the door.

'Come in,' he said. 'The other girls are here.'

'Really?'

'Of course not, Ted.'

'Is Anthony home?'

'No. But come in. Have a drink. I haven't slept at all. I've got the football on.'

I heard it, the crowd noise of a Premier League game. 'It's okay,' I replied. 'I'm going home to bed.'

Jens didn't want me to go. 'What is it?'

'Oh, I had a question for him.' It was a bitter one; the last thing to do was reveal it. 'I wanted to know how he could sleep with other girls.'

'Go home,' said Jens. 'It's not your question.'

19

Dad rang to say he was visiting. He and Dr Andrews were going to devise a course on maritime law together. We should have dinner while he was in town. When he phoned again to say he'd arrived, he told me to come over to his hotel first. He had something for me.

People often find ghosts in photographs, but my experience that afternoon was that the ghost inhabited the person holding it. The way he lost my mother was inhaled again, as he gave me the photograph and breathed another farewell.

'I don't want you to give it to me,' I said.

'I'd like you to have it,' he answered.

'I'd rather you told me about her. To me, that's more important. I feel like I hardly know her, even though she's such a big part of our life – well, your life. You hold on to her memory, but you don't share it.'

'You wrote to me about Claire. You asked me about letting her go.' He stopped. 'I don't know why people are in such a rush to let go.'

'They want to be happy,' I said. 'They can't be happy together.'

'Can't they?'

'They each want to start a new life.'

'There's no such thing as a new life, Ted,' he said. 'That doesn't mean people can't be happy.'

It was three months since I'd seen Claire, and since her and Anthony's break-up. I felt that Anthony had been avoiding me, too. He didn't answer his phone. I walked from the hotel to the college, and then I rang her at home to ask if she'd join me and Dad for dinner later that evening. I said I needed the company.

'Are you sure you want to take me?' she asked.

'Of course.'

'There's plenty I could say to your father.'

'I thought you were angry at me, not him.'

'Yes. Actually, yes, much more angry at you.'

'Why?'

'You don't call for three months and then ask me to have dinner with your dad.'

'I had to wait.'

'Maybe I should make you wait, as well,' she said.

She didn't, though. She agreed to come to dinner at Ming's, an over-large room of plastic tablecloths and cardboard kittens. My father had long loved it, and wanted to eat there at least once every time he came to Sydney. That evening, we ate early, before the large families arrived and crowded the place with the reassuring noises of old relationships and conversation. We sat at the end of one of the long tables, like the only ones on a bus, hoping there might soon be other early commuters.

My father was ageing, but I liked it in him. There were new, bronze creases in his neck and across his hands; I wondered if I seemed older to him, too – I was about to turn twenty-two and I thought I could see the difference. Anthony was right about my father: he could sometimes look dusty. Especially when he travelled.

But this time he even seemed to be wearing the clothes he'd driven down in; it was unusual for him not to change before dinner, for his early-evening rituals of a gin and a cigar. Perhaps because of the emptiness of the restaurant, we sat more closely than we usually would.

'I've been busy in the garden,' he said to Claire. 'Actually, I've got some questions for your father. I'm sure he'd be able to help me.'

Claire released none of the anger that she'd hinted at, and which in person seemed to have an uncertain target, Dad or me, or perhaps Anthony. She touched Dad's arm in that way of her mother's, and said he should phone her father. 'He'd love to hear from you.' And then, 'Dad used to tease me that I'd marry Ted one day.'

'I can't believe that,' I said.

'I'm still counting on you taking care of me,' she said quickly, her tone uncertain.

That seemed a rather distant promise now. 'Jens thinks I should be a diplomat. He says there are excellent subjects in Copenhagen. It sounds good. I can do them in English.' I watched Claire, but she didn't meet my eyes. When she did look up, it was to check my father's response.

'I'm not sure how it would benefit you,' he said. 'You're better off going straight into practice here.'

'Wouldn't you pay?' I asked, suddenly angry. 'I doubt I'll be ready to start work next year.'

'This is turning out to be an expensive dinner,' he said to Claire. Then to me, evenly, 'I've spoken to some friends. There are firms that will take you, even though your marks aren't at the top.'

'I don't know. I think the marks are the point.'

'The point?'

'I think they tell me exactly what I should be doing next year. The only subject I've done well in is International. Not much point hanging around here, is there?'

I didn't know where my unpleasantness was coming from. Across me had swept an anger that I'd only seen in Anthony and Claire, never in myself. I felt it drawing me to a position that had very little to do with what I really wanted.

Thankfully, the food came out. Dad wasn't one to stand down from an argument, or to quiet me – he was too calm for either. But perhaps for Claire's sake he watched the food being served and said, 'We can talk about this tomorrow, if you're serious about going.'

I couldn't drop it. 'Why wait?' I wanted a win, in some ways against them both, but in other ways against my father only – a performance for Claire, for the princess and peasant daughter both. 'Claire, would you prefer it if we talked about this later?'

'Would you do what I asked?'

'Yes, you know that.'

'In that case, stop talking and just say you'll stay in Sydney with us.'

'With you?'

'With us.'

'There you are,' said my father. 'You've been told.'

Claire had now finished art college. But, even more than me, she resisted the next step, into work, whatever that meant for someone like her. Her parents sent money so that she could stay on in Sydney, but soon she'd have to go back to the farm if nothing came up in town. Anthony, I heard, had gone from waiting tables in the Cross to working as a salesman in a Rose Bay art gallery that occasionally hung his paintings. Jens told me this, for Anthony still didn't want to meet. When I finally did catch him on his mobile, he said he'd write to me soon.

'Anthony, I live around the corner.'

'So?'

'Can't we just meet up?'

'I'm at the gallery day and night.'

'Are you saying you're too busy?'

'Have you seen Claire?' he asked.

'Yes.'

'I haven't seen her.'

'I know. You're going to have to talk at some point.'

There was a silence. 'Are you okay, Ted?'

'Let's meet,' I insisted.

'I'm writing first. I want to write to you. Like when you were still home. Say hello to Claire.'

Mostly, she spent her mornings invisible. Neither she nor the others in the house seemed willing to answer the phone before lunch, as though that were when a calling time should begin, the drawing room finally revealed. In the afternoons, when at last there was enough movement in the world to stir them, she came out to shop, or catch a bus to Clovelly or Bronte.

After our dinner with my father, I took to meeting her for these beach trips. On the bus together, we still talked mainly about Anthony, but also her paintings and the girls she lived with. They seemed to be like her – beautiful, a little angry but also busy and ambitious for their art, at least in the afternoons and evenings when the light was feline enough for the girls to appear. I told her that my father and Dr Andrews were working together.

I joked about what a funny pair they were. In reply, Claire asked whether I'd met anyone nice. I said, 'Of course I have. Law girls are easy.'

'Bastard,' she said. 'Nicer than me?'

'Much nicer than you.'

'Why do you come to the beach with me, then, and not them?'

'Historical reasons.' She hit me on the leg. Before I could think better of it, I asked, 'You didn't leave Anthony because of me, did you?'

'No.'

'Then why?'

'I couldn't stay.' She checked herself, and then said, 'That's all.'

'You still love him, don't you?'

'We both still love him,' she told me.

We arrived at Bronte and sat on a bench that overlooked tanned rocks and oval pools. Her landscape studies, like her studies of people, were still never quite finished. She set them aside before they could appear complete, so they might always be mere sketches – of the direction of the wind, the spray off the crest of the waves, the bends in the top trees after storms. These days she used only pencils or charcoal. I asked if I could keep some of her work, for I thought she would otherwise have thrown much of it away. She said yes, but she didn't want me to frame them or hang them up.

One evening, when we got back from the beach later than usual and I walked her from the bus stop to her place, she took my hand. 'The others are out,' she said.

I hadn't been inside the house before. Her bedroom wasn't a room of its own, exactly, but part of a long veranda that had been closed and converted. The street-side was walled in by a stretch of glass – purple and green squares. They were opaque, but the headlights of the cars outside crossed the room in arcs of coloured movement.

The light found her body. Between cars, she disappeared again into the shadow of the room, and I found myself waiting for the traffic, waiting to see her. Moving over to me, she leant forward to kiss me. Then she straightened herself, sitting upright.

'I love you,' I said.

'I know. We love each other.'

'I'm yours.'

'No,' she answered, 'not yet.'

'Come here.'

'I can't see you. It's dark.' She leant forward to kiss me again, and covered my face in her thick hair, as if to block the lights of the next car to come down the street outside. She said, 'I need you closer.'

20

Nine years after we'd met, Claire and I swapped an enduring clarity for our first awkwardness. What was there to say next? There didn't seem to be a natural question and answer to follow the night we'd had, and the short, light hours of sleep afterwards. It was six; we had coffee together in her bedroom of sixties morning colours – light like tiles – and perhaps we both thought about how long we'd waited for this moment, but most acutely whether we'd waited long enough. We hardly spoke till I said goodbye. I wouldn't see her again until long after the next thing that happened, which for a while felt like the only thing that had ever happened between us.

That day, I rang Anthony and insisted that we meet. I told him that Claire and I had made love. I told him how it had happened, after a day at the beach, at her place. He blushed, but it wasn't exactly anger, more an awareness that he'd been caught out by his own expectations. 'How was it?' he asked.

'It was beautiful.'

'At last.' Correcting himself, the strangled tone of that phrase, he added, 'I'm not jealous. I can't be jealous of you.' He looked at me to discover whether I believed him. We both saw something else: it was a hope that he still had her, even after she'd been with me, and a change in how he saw his own future. 'I suppose this means it's really over,' he said, as much a question as a statement. 'She won't come back to me now. Did you stay the night?'

'Yes.'

'Did you make love again in the morning?'

'No.'

'She didn't want to?'

'It was different in the morning,' I said. I was ready to tell him anything he wanted. 'Or, we were back to where we were. It felt obvious we weren't about to start anything. You know she still loves you.'

He ignored this. 'I'm glad you told me,' he said. 'Always kind, Ted.'

'Have I hurt you?'

'No. You haven't. I've been waiting for this. It's a relief that it's come. I hope you haven't hurt each other. You think she's still in love with me. I'd say you're much too in love with her.'

'I don't even know what that means.'

'You should know, Ted. By now you should know.'

His letter to me came bundled with sketches and postcards, as always more than just the matter at hand. He delivered this one, gave it to me one afternoon, and told me to open it when I got back to college, not before.

I did as I was told.

When I read it now, late at night sitting back in my father's study, I find myself more terrified, shocked than I was at the time. Now, it seems so clear that he was in deep distress, and that this wasn't merely another poem, another picture, another of Anthony's performances. The day I received it, it simply seemed every bit an Anthony kind of letter.

Ted, would you let me go because I'm not happy here. With so much cruelty around us, I'm lying by staying. I've always thought of the end of my life as a gentle thing. I want no part of the violence, the whole manliness here. And I feel so utterly alone. Sometimes I need you so much that I almost feel you here. I need you here. All we get is men who need to be men, need to show how great they are. I'm not above or below it. I'm standing beside it and I'm frightened that if I step to the right I'll be like him and if I step to the left I'll be like him and if I walk straight down the middle his path will still cross mine. So I want to stand still and just watch him walk by me. I want you and Claire to let me go. I'd rather die now as I am than die like him. Please say yes. Please let me go.

I folded the letter and placed it back with the drawings that had accompanied it, and spent the next morning at the law library, determined to put it out of my mind. I wouldn't even call. But at lunch, I went back to my room. I needed to read the letter again. Then I walked with it to Anthony's place. I would make him take it back, refute it.

I found him in the café next door, at a corner table. He'd finished a coffee, but sat smoking, watching the traffic.

'Why this?' I held out the letter.

'Nothing's changed,' he replied. 'I've had enough.'

I sat down beside him. I still wasn't sure what I was witnessing. 'You have to see your way out of this. You change all the time. Some days you're so full of hope. Remember that. Some days all we do is laugh.'

He wasn't listening. 'Ted, I'm having a dinner party tonight. I want you to come. I've called Claire. She says she won't come. I need you there, though. I need at least one of you there.'

'You can't do this to her.'

'You have each other now.'

'Stop this. Do you really think we could be together if you did this?'

'Will you come, Ted?' he asked. 'I'm going to cook a beautiful meal. I want you to be there.'

'Forget the dinner and come for a walk. Let's catch a train somewhere. Let's go to the Blue Mountains. I'll phone Claire.'

'I've said goodbye to her.'

At least they'd spoken, I thought. 'She doesn't believe you, then.'

'No, she doesn't believe me. Do you?'

'Of course not.'

He put out his cigarette and tried to seem indifferent. 'Come shopping with me for dinner, or you can go. It doesn't matter. But you should come tonight. You should be there. I want to say goodbye, even if you won't give me what I want. You can do that for me. You can say goodbye.'

It was a revolting idea. 'I'm not coming to this dinner,' I told him. 'Claire was right to say no.'

'You don't think I have the right to leave?'

'No. We love you. You only have the right to stay.'

'I can't tell you everything. Come to dinner. I want you to be happy, Ted. You deserve it. You're so good. You and Claire are perfect together.'

'No,' I said and stood up. I left him; I couldn't stay any longer. I left him there, and as I walked away I decided that I'd had enough, too. Of Claire, as well – of the endless, humiliating attempts to find something of myself in them. I wouldn't go to the dinner; I wouldn't call Claire; I wouldn't take it seriously.

But when I got back to college, I tried straight away to reach her. She wasn't home. A housemate said she'd gone to the farm.

'The farm? Really?'

'Yes.'

'When?'

'She took the train last night.'

Then an afternoon that formed into tight circles, each trying to push its way out, and drawn back in. I needed to walk. I went down to the lower ovals, thinking of Claire, my mind working too hard, realising that I had to go to this dinner after all, for Claire was on the farm, and one of us had to go. It would be alright.

The evening came, the circles closing again around an obscene ceremony. I arrived at eight, saw four of them sitting in a huddle on beanbags, smoking hash, Anthony and three from art college, new friends who said they understood this moment, this act – said it was brave: it was a beautiful thing, to leave in this way, at peace. They beatified Anthony. The Anthony who had seen only beauty in Claire, and none in himself. Is that all this was, I thought: everyone needing someone they didn't understand?

I was overwhelmed with hatred, at last. I hated him: the false intellectualism, the cannabis, the smoke in the front room; high, grey windows without curtains, and candles in the black reflection. I couldn't stay in the living room with his friends. I went to the kitchen and tried to think of a sentence to break the whole thing, to cut the circle across its axis.

He joined me and asked what music we should put on. He'd brought out some of my opera records, and asked me to choose one.

'Don't be ridiculous. We're not listening to opera,' I said. 'I'm not staying. I can't stand this.'

He was too stoned to acknowledge the ugliness; he saw only emotion. 'It's so important to me that you came,' he said. 'You're the only one I need here.'

'I don't believe you,' I replied. 'You'd stop this if you needed me.'

'I love you, Ted. Come and join the others.'

'No.'

'We'll eat soon. I've nearly finished cooking.'

'Where's Jens?'

'He's in New Zealand. I haven't told him. I didn't think it would be fair.'

'Nothing about this is fair,' I said.

'Go and sit down.' Anthony smiled, told me to relax and have a good time – that's all he wanted now, for all of us to enjoy our last night together. He said he was happy, finally happy.

'No.' I sat down at the kitchen bench and waited, watched him cook, his back to me. It was all a performance, one of his Gothic masks. 'Don't do this,' I said. 'Don't even act it.'

He came over to me and held me. 'Kindness, Ted. That's what you don't see, but I do. It's all that matters, all that I care about now. I've been waiting and now I can go. This isn't a sad night.'

'This is what you call beauty?'

'Now that you're here.'

In that case, I wanted to make it ugly; force the scars into the room before they were glamorised by reflection and thought. Leave. I wouldn't stay. 'This is awful. Do you think this is any way to treat us?'

'I don't know.'

'You want to leave with everything.'

'No.'

'Fuck you.'

And then finally a column of clean air in the smoke. 'I'm sorry,' he said at last. 'It wasn't right to ask you to come.'

I told him I was leaving. He took my hand, led me into his bedroom.

'Kiss me,' he said. 'Kiss me once, properly.'

I kissed him on the lips. 'That was a brother's kiss,' he said, 'but I'll take it. Go home, Ted. I want to go to bed. I feel stupid.'

He tried to stand up, steady himself, but he fell back onto the bed. I moved closer to him, leant over him. 'Promise me.'

'I promise.' His hands were on my face and he laughed. 'I've changed my mind.' He fixed his eyes on me and said it again: 'I promise. Really. You can go. I know how much you hate them.'

'Yes.'

'Thank God you came.'

'I hate the way they encourage you.'

He laughed again. 'I'll get new ones. I'm sick of them.'

'And remember your old ones.' I held him and said, 'Do you promise?'

'Yes. I promise. I promise. I'm better. You have to go. I'm so tired.'

I stepped outside with the feeling I was filming myself walking home. It was dark and raining, most of the orange lamplight held in the wet streets. If I observed the scene from far enough away, I could be convinced by what he'd said; it was all nothing more than another melodrama, another letter from Anthony, another poem. Performance. As I reached the end of Glebe Point Road, I thought that he was mainly just cruel, and that I couldn't bear his cruelty any longer.

But the side of me that watched the film also saw something truer. I saw it, didn't I? Through the disbelief and anger, still it was there. He wanted to go and I wasn't stopping him.

The group stayed up until two, apparently, I suppose only for another couple of hours after I left. It seems they still spoke openly about what Anthony had planned, but now they wanted him to stop. A debate: leaving was beautiful, but was it too hurtful to those who loved him? Yes, he'd changed his mind. All he felt now was tiredness. He wanted his own bed. They could go. That was between one and two, or around the same time I fell asleep. They were sure they'd talked him out of it, that life had claimed him, not death. They wanted to go out, to dance, and so they left him on his own.

I woke just before five, and knew. The sky and sea had merged and fallen apart again, the last circle of night when the horizon forms again. I knew. Anthony was dead; my mother was dead: the same idea that belonged only in silence, behind the spoken. *You're too late.* The weakness in the legs, in the steps I took to close the circle, from college to Glebe Point Road, past the boarded-up grocers, the café with its grille pulled down.

The front door was unlocked. I ran inside, down the hall to his bedroom, and found him lying on his back. He'd taken pills and cut his wrists. A thick red stain on the sheet, on either side of his body, and red drops on the grey floorboards. Blood in pencil lines along the gaps in the timbers. His eyes were closed. I kissed him, and wished there was less beauty in the world, less art. I sat with him, and asked my mother to take care of him. I asked him to forgive me.

21

Anthony died on 12 November, a month before my twenty-second birthday. I rang Dad, and told him that I'd spent the day at the hospital and the police station, and then caught the bus back to college.

'Come home,' he said. 'The funeral will be here, I'm sure.'

'Yes.'

'Have you called Claire?'

I said I'd phoned her first, from the hospital. 'She wouldn't come to the phone. Her dad answered.'

'She'd guessed?'

'Yes. I got the feeling from Nikolas that she guessed as soon as I rang.'

Dad said again it was time for me to come home. I shouldn't stay in Sydney. He'd come and get me.

'I want to stay with him,' I replied.

I said I'd catch the train the next day, but in the morning Dad called to say he was waiting for me downstairs. I found him in the dining hall. I didn't cry, not then, but as soon as I saw him I put my head against his shoulder. I wanted that part of him, the perfect hollow that belonged to me, and was there even when Claire and Anthony were gone. The sense of him being with me.

'I was worried you might stay,' he said. 'It wouldn't help to be here any longer.'

'I've got one more exam.'

'I've talked to Andrews. He says you've done enough for a pass. Take the pass and come home with me. We'll leave after you've had something to eat.'

It occurred to me that Dad had been driving all night. 'Aren't you tired?'

'I had a good run down.'

We left the college and walked out into the low sky of a Sydney morning, watched how it reached down and joined the traffic up George Street, insisted on another start.

But by evening, when we reached Lion's Head, the sky remained blurred by that reluctant haze in the last hours by the beach. Claire phoned to say she wouldn't come to the funeral. She couldn't.

Nor did Anthony's father come. His mother was there, and twenty others. Only two went up to the coffin, Eric and my father. I found I couldn't manage it, but Dad said he'd place my copy of the Dickinson inside. He asked, 'Is there anything you want me to say to him?'

You had no right to go. You have destroyed us both. Claire hasn't come, did you expect that she would? She won't say goodbye. What have you found, something better?

'Say that we love him,' I replied.

When we got home, Dad asked me to join him for a drink in the study. It was a long time since the two of us had sat there, but all the same I half-expected him to start work, as he used to. I would have been happy with that, to sip on a tea with a splash of scotch and watch him at his desk, listen to the odd remark he wanted to make about a case, one that at last he could expect me to understand.

He took his familiar place at the desk by the window, but instead of working, he turned to me and said, 'I think we should visit Claire tomorrow.'

'I'm not sure,' I replied. 'If she wanted to see me, she would have come.'

'I don't think that's it. My guess is that she wanted to see you, but she couldn't stand to go to the funeral.'

'She should've come.'

'Why don't we drive up to the farm in the morning.'

I agreed, but in the glowing morning I left the house early, and walked along the beach towards Nambucca, all the way to the estuary. It was an uninterrupted horizon of sand, and then the water as reflection alone, without depth. I thought about how good it would be not to have to turn around. There was something in that thought that I understood about Anthony, but not enough to pierce the reflection, the strangeness that shone on the surface.

Tears came. It was the first time I'd cried since I was a child, and started as a choked coughing, as though I were out of practice. I looked away from the sea, so that an empty beach might witness it, the way the shock insisted on a display. And then I stopped and stood at the water's edge, and for a moment felt as though I was stopping everything. That it was possible. There was an origin point here, at the shoreline, that could always be returned to as a finality.

I walked back to the house, my thoughts cleared by the false solace of tears and blue water. Happiness came, an odd pleasure that lay at the beginning of grief. The energy given to the ones left to mourn. I wondered if Claire would feel it, too. Would she admit to some relief?

The following day I rang her and said goodbye for a second time, and for a second time I offered to leave her be, my strange way of asking her to come to me, to help me through this. Dad overheard the conversation, and later that afternoon said he was willing to send me to Denmark for a year, to join Jens in the course there, the one we knew would be a waste of time, and what I needed most.

On the phone, I asked Claire if she needed that sort of time. She answered, 'Maybe that's best. Maybe it's best if you go away. I think it'll help you.'

22

Jens had returned to Copenhagen a couple of weeks ahead of me, leaving New Zealand and stopping just long enough in Sydney to close the house. He met me at the airport and drove me into town. It was mid-January – when Christmas had been and gone, and days were merely a pulse of white light between nine and three. But in the shop windows and the cafés, in the lanes between the long mall and its parallel streets of locked-up bikes and painted rails, there was also companionable warmth.

Jens and I would be taking the same postgraduate course in international law. 'Our first class is tomorrow,' he said.

'Yes.'

'Don't worry about being late. Sources of international law. We'll spend the day learning that there aren't any.'

It was two months since Anthony's funeral, but I hadn't seen Jens since before the dinner party. 'I didn't think you'd ever leave Sydney,' he said.

'Why?'

'Because of Claire. Have you seen her?'

'No. She went back to the farm. I think she'll be there for a while.'

'You visited her there?'

'No.'

'You haven't seen her?'

'No.'

'Welcome to Denmark, then,' he said. 'You should be fine. This is the one part of the world where we deal with suicide as badly as you have.'

'Is that it, then?' I said. 'Is that your line on me?'

He took a hand off the steering wheel and gripped my arm. 'I'm your friend.'

'Yes.'

I didn't want to talk. He went on, 'I'm trying to be funny. It's because I don't know what to say.'

'I'm not sure what I'm doing here,' I replied.

'We'll find out, then.'

In Sydney, Jens had seemed too assured for us, or for the group he'd chosen. In Copenhagen, however, he seemed perfectly adapted to the narrow streets, the sweep of girls on bikes, slow drinkers outside, bright windows and white shops. He had the Scandinavian way of being odd while also clearly belonging to the establishment. But he insisted he was a radical. Sometimes, he swore he wanted the whole machine brought down. But in all other ways – maybe even in this way – he was being deeply social. When he said the types of things Anthony had said, it was merely disarming, as though he were complimenting the machine by saying it needed destroying.

He was putting on weight, and it suited him. Most days, he seemed to drink only coffee until lunch and then beer until midnight. I never saw him drink anything else, never water. His hair was growing with him, and got redder as it got longer and saw less of the sun.

For the first time, I liked him completely and unguardedly. If in Sydney I'd befriended him for Anthony's sake, now I wanted more than anything to be around someone who was Anthony's opposite – someone less vulnerable, and yet less impenetrable. I was quite sure this covered Jens, even if, like Anthony, he wore his opinions loudly. He'd joined the Socialist Party, and each week we met and smoked a great deal of pot and cigarettes, and organised demonstrations. And they ran an English-language reading group. That year, Jens said, we'd cover Dante, Wordsworth and Ibsen. At the end of the year, we'd probably return to Dante.

Fine. I thought I was probably a socialist, too. I had learnt about art from Anthony's friends, and perhaps I could learn about politics from Jens's. I loved the authors that were being covered. Perhaps, as Jens argued, they were radical authors, proto-socialists. So I nodded when Jens and the others said that everything was political. At my request, as a tangent we read *Ich und Du*, a German philosophical work that I'd met through Anthony's and Dad's reading about Dag Hammarskjöld, who'd been translating the text into Swedish at the time of his death. It was about understanding God through the meetings we have with the people around us, and had influenced some of Hammarskjöld's thinking about God and political interventions.

The day after the reading group, Jens was impatient to tell me what he really thought of the text. 'Some people are waiting for God to tap them on the shoulder and say, "Here it is. Here's what I want you to give your life for. From now on, you can leave yourself and your desires behind. You now have the shield of duty." Do you see what a privileged view that is? Not everyone gets that tap on the shoulder. God leaves a hell of a lot of people alone. What are they supposed to do?'

I replied that people weren't to blame if they were part of the upper classes, or if they had opportunities to do good work. 'You're not so badly off, Jens.'

'No one escapes privilege, it runs too deep,' agreed Jens. 'It's why we wait. We expect something will come.' I thought of Dad. He'd been waiting for twenty years, satisfied with reading and writing until he could join my mother. Jens added, 'By the way you shouldn't expect Claire to wait for you, either. You should write. Or call her.'

The truth was that I didn't know what to say. At night, after class and the obligatory beers with Jens, I began to draft letters that seemed to say nothing unless they could say it all, and I wasn't sure that either of us wanted everything said. What had been our part in Anthony's death? I went to sleep with the question, and woke with the certainty that I dreamt of Anthony and Claire, but I couldn't remember – only that dreams of them kept returning, followed by the same untidy feeling, as though I'd forgotten to do something important, a promise I'd made before coming to Denmark.

I left my college room and took to the city as I'd once taken to the sea: a space where I searched for things I believed in but didn't fully comprehend. Darkness brought it into relief, the white x-ray lines between the black spaces. At least, I felt more present in the shadows between the lamplights and the odd corner bar that remained open. I walked in the early hours, and stopped on my way back, drawn in by music. I found different international laws: mainly, the laws of loneliness – you can always talk to someone who's working; you should always find something to read, even if you don't plan to do any reading, no matter the time; sit by the window, even if it means you're on show, because the quiet spots in the corners are, by natural law, reserved for couples.

Dad wrote regularly by email, and sometimes I sat with my laptop and read over our correspondence. He asked how I was doing on my own. I said I was keeping busy and that I loved Copenhagen. I didn't really know what else to say, but I wanted him to feel that coming away had been the right decision.

Jens has been taking good care of me since I arrived. We haven't talked much about Anthony, except when I first arrived, and I'm sure that's for the best at the moment. There isn't much class time, but the reading is intensive, and I like the routine of sitting in the library or in the coffee shops reading articles.

I bought a bike the other day. It isn't far to ride from the student apartments down to the water. The sea's grey and some days very dark, always very different from the colour of the sea at home.

On cold days, the wind comes in from the north. But even then there are people out walking and riding along the shoreline, and tourists following the signs out to the statue of the Little Mermaid.

I feel close to Mum here. I have her picture on my bedside table. And I've been thinking about Whitby, and maybe visiting while I'm here. What do you think? There are cheap flights from here to Manchester, and I'm sure I have the time to get away for a week. I could visit Lillie. I know she's wanted us to come back.

Dad replied that he hoped we'd go back together one day, but that he understood if I took the chance to go now. I was so close, after all.

*

Jens never mentioned or visited his family, but I knew they were barely part of his life. He lived apart from them in a rebel suburb, Christiania. I didn't ever meet a girlfriend, or friends outside the reading group. If he wasn't with us readers, or at one of the rallies that he helped to organise, he was at a café drinking and smoking, seemingly waiting for me to round the corner so we could argue.

The reading group valorised argument above all else. In this, our conversations were led by a middle-aged literary scholar called Peter Jorgensen. Peter was a star among the radical community, and rather good at being an enigmatic one. He'd interrupt discussions of Dante with questions that didn't appear to have anything to do with hell, but somehow might reveal our understanding of the text nonetheless. Early in spring, when we sat outdoors at a café in one of the narrowing corners of Studiestræde, he asked us to describe the colour of the evening sky.

I gave a bland response; something like, the sky was nectarine. The others ignored it. Then Jens said it was that dull colour between leaving something good and arriving somewhere worse – and that true damnation lay with the faint hope that remains even once a good thing is lost. The others all had a go at improving on that. After that night, I was less regular. I told Jens that I didn't like the reading group.

'What do you like, then?' he asked. 'Just the people you already know?'

It seemed it was finally time for us to talk about Anthony and Claire again. 'I'm confused, Jens. You know that. But I know there's no finding something new, something clean. You don't get to start again.'

'You can't put it behind you, either.'

'Exactly.'

Jens asked, 'Do you hate him?'

'Sometimes,' I replied. 'When I go to bed, the last thing at night. I've prayed for him. I've told him I hate him. Sometimes it's the last thing I say. Isn't that awful? To go to sleep with that thought.'

'He gave you a lot. He made you a better person.'

'I don't believe that. He showed me that I'm weak. Is that an improvement?'

'You didn't fail him.'

'I feel so sick about it,' I said.

'Is it guilt?'

'Yes. Maybe. Or disbelief. I can't believe that it's happened. I want there to be something to do, some way of taking it away. I want to turn around and find that I'm wrong. He isn't dead at all.'

Jens lit a cigarette. He offered me one, too, and I took it. 'I don't like smoking in the wind,' I said.

'Have one anyway.'

'I can't accept that he's gone. Even though the pain is there. Even though I was the one who found him. I expect to be able to stop it.'

'He shouldn't have let you find him.'

'I don't know. What difference does that make? I left him. It's only right that I found him.'

'That's probably true,' said Jens. We finished our cigarettes; they burnt away quickly. He added, 'I'm sorry if I'm pushing you too hard.'

I could see that Jens didn't think we'd spoken enough. He could make his point, that the mistake now was leaving Claire. But I knew that already. He said, 'I'll tell you what's obvious. You'll wait forever. You'll spend the rest of your life halfway between Anthony and Claire.' He paused, and then concluded, 'I think that's why you're in Copenhagen. This is a good place to drift.'

*

In summer, when the reading group took a break, Jens disappeared, too; none of us saw him around town. Copenhagen felt empty, for he was such a regular at the bars, and my new friends – the ones I'd made for myself – only ever appeared in the last hours before dawn, when even Peter and the reading-group regulars were at home in their studio apartments.

When Jens finally returned a fortnight later, he phoned to tell me he was back. Could we meet at the university? It sounded urgent; he wanted me to come downtown straight away. I rushed out the door, and found him leaning against a spare section of steel rail – the only part unclaimed by chains and bicycle handlebars.

'What's the matter?' I asked him.

'I need a drink.'

For a while, I thought he meant he needed a drink before he could tell me what was on his mind. But gradually I realised that he just wanted a drink; that was the emergency. We followed the slow bends of Strøget and found a bar. 'I've been ill,' he said. 'Don't tell the others, but I had to pass gallstones. It was terrible. Jesus.'

I couldn't help but laugh. 'Did you go home?'

'Go home? Why would I go home? You think that's a better place to shit gallstones?'

'Some people like to have family around when they're unwell.'

'Yes, that's right.' He sipped his beer. 'Thank God for beer. My doctor asked, "How much coffee do you drink?" I told her, "Hey, I'm Danish."' Jens held his hands up. 'Anyway, I've been around the whole time, hiding from you and the others.'

There was a pause. 'Is this what you wanted to tell me, Jens? About your gallstones? Is that why we had to come out for a beer?'

'You don't care?'

'I care about you. Your gallstones, I don't know.'

'Why do we bother, you and me?' he said. 'Eh?' I wasn't sure why we wouldn't bother – we liked each other and we shared a past. But Jens was impatient, and something in me made him notice all our differences.

At last he gave me what was on his mind. He said he'd used his time away to think about my defining weakness.

'Thanks, Jens.'

'Alright. Here's what I've got for you. If you want something, you have to push. You have to push someone else out of the way. Do you know how to do that? Here, I'll show you.'

Jens reached forward and pushed me off my chair.

'Jens!' I shouted at him.

A group at the next table stood up, to help me or to get out of the way. Jens persuaded them that it was alright, we were friends. He reached down to help me up. 'I've wanted to do that for some time,' he said.

'Why?'

'The three of you made such a fucking mess of it.' He said it sympathetically, as though the push and this conversation had been all for me, and also for Anthony and Claire. I didn't know how to respond. We still had the attention of the next table. I tried to imitate Jens's manner of making the moment seem natural, but I half-expected another assault.

'Is this your way of telling me to leave?' I said.

A waiter came over, a belated reaction to what was almost a fight. Jens laughed, and told him, 'I've been sober for two weeks. I need beer.' He ordered a round. When the drinks came to the table, he turned to me and asked, as though we'd just met, 'Are you enjoying life in Copenhagen?'

'Jesus, Jens, are you high on something?'

'I asked you a simple question. Are you enjoying my city?'

'It's a great place.'

'You feel like you're learning something?'

'Yes,' I answered. 'I'm learning about Danish manners.'

He looked tired now. When he stared out of the front window, I noticed that he'd lost some weight in the face. He turned back to me. 'When you came to the door that morning, and asked me to fetch Anthony, I guess I found out for sure that you were in love with Claire. I thought that was okay. But you were asking all the wrong questions. You were thinking about Anthony. You have to push him out of the way now, and ask the question you wanted to ask that night.'

'What was that?' I said.

'You don't know? Of course you do. You wanted to ask Anthony if Claire was in love with you.'

'Why couldn't I ask her?' I wondered aloud.

'Right. Same reason you're here,' said Jens. 'You don't believe she's yours. And now there's no Anthony to tell you. Only me.'

'And who'd believe you?'

But I did believe most of what Jens had to say. Perhaps watching my father settling for a life of books and the patched light of the study had convinced me that eventually you had to go out and see what was there. At the same time, I knew how to delay. I loved Dad's stillness, and I trusted it. That's what Jens saw and what he wanted to push out of me.

I had decided not to go to Whitby. However close it was – a ferry ride across the North Sea – most of all I wanted to go with Dad. It seemed almost an impossible journey without him. For I knew that

I wanted to go there in order to understand him, and our life in Australia, as much as to find Mum.

Jens had found a job – he would be joining the Danish foreign office. Our last night together started at the reading group, which I'd rejoined in earnest after Jens told me I was being too precious about Peter and his enigmatic questions. Afterwards Jens and I walked out together. Instead of returning to college, we took our regular diversion along Strøget to the end, and then stepped down into Ernst Hviid's, a tourist bar that was quiet that night. I liked it down there in the basement rooms. The windows were at eye level, and we watched the street pass by from the knee down. It snowed, and then rained. A line of brown slush against the bottom window panes.

He ordered food and beer, and when our drinks arrived declared a toast. 'I doubt we'll see each other again,' he said, smiling fondly. It was said with his usual goodwill. 'People drift apart.'

'Maybe that's true,' I replied.

'She's yours if you want her. Your future is with her.'

'Have you ever written to her?'

'Yes. I wrote her by email a couple of times.'

'Did she write back?'

'No.'

'Never mind,' I said. There was no point writing to Claire. She never replied.

Jens had saved a last attempt at drawing me in. 'Don't you want to ask me what I wrote to her?'

'I'm sure it was very sensitive, Jens,' I said. 'You've got such a way with words. I just hope you didn't lecture her as much as you do me.'

'Well, here it is. My sensitivity. I wrote: *Don't think you could have stopped him. You didn't know what he would do.* That's right, isn't it, Ted? You didn't think he would go ahead with it.'

I admitted to Jens that on the night of the dinner party I'd felt Anthony had wanted me to stay. That some part of me heard an unspoken request. He'd needed me there to stop him.

Jens kept eating and didn't look at me. At last he spoke. 'You shouldn't have left, then,' he said, 'not if you knew. He might have made it through the night.'

'He said he'd changed his mind. I believed him. Or part of me believed him. And then – I couldn't sit there any longer. I hated them. I hated the performance, what he was doing for them.'

Jens pushed his food away. 'Did you let them decide?'

'No.'

'Remember, Ted, you don't have a cold heart.'

I'd never heard Jens mention the heart before. It sounded strange spoken by someone as warm-hearted as him. 'I wish I hadn't left him.'

'Go home, then.'

23

It was late October. With Jens gone I felt stuck in that early-winter month, in a Copenhagen with a left-behind feeling. I ran out of money and emailed Dad, asking for help. He replied that he'd lend me as much as I needed, but added that he thought he'd have a better chance of getting his money back if it went into setting me up in Sydney, rather than towards another month in Europe. He knew I was applying for jobs in international firms. In fact, I was down to my last interview before giving up and phoning home.

Dad said it'd be a week before he could get me on an earlier flight home. I had only a couple of hundred dollars left in my account, so he organised some extra money and bought me a train pass as an early birthday present. If I wasn't going to Whitby, I should see some of the countryside nearby. There was no point just waiting.

I started with the night train to Stockholm. I shared a cabin with an engineer who wanted to hear all I could tell him about Australia – he'd always wanted to live there, go somewhere you could be outside every day of the year. I told him about the sea, and how in Australia it completely absorbed the colour of the sky. I told him that in Sydney you felt it everywhere you went: it was a town where the sea and the sky seemed to meet at the end of every road.

'You miss it?' he asked.

'Yes. I'm on my way back now.'

We kept talking for a couple of hours, until I couldn't stay awake any longer. It was past one. When we drew into Stockholm terminus at five, my companion translated an announcement on the intercom telling passengers they could stay on board until seven. I slept for another hour, and then walked with my pack through the station and out into a morning that was colder than Copenhagen's. The train had arrived in an off-centre, gloomy part of the city shaded by overpasses. But I found the water and then the cafés that opened for the morning commuters.

I sat at a window seat and took measured sips of coffee. I didn't want my cup taken away. Efficient girls in black aprons were a bit of a curse in such moments; they were unremitting in their tidying up. Outside, the self-possession and swift purpose of the Swedes made the time I had seem indulgent. *You should get up and work*, it said. *Do something.* So I tore a page from my journal and began writing to Claire, even if there was no point, and even if she never answered letters. I gave her my thoughts about Copenhagen and some of Jens's news. I told her that I knew he'd written and what he'd said, and that she should write to congratulate him on a job he'd managed to get, despite himself.

Half an hour later, I moved coffee shops and tried to continue the letter; I remember a line about seeing her the last time before Anthony died, and how heavy and vacant of any real meaning the line was. What could I tell her about losing him? What did it matter how she'd seemed to me those last weeks before he left, or during the night she and I had had together?

So I tore up the letter and began again. This time, I wrote that I hadn't wanted to leave her. I was thinking about her sketches, and how this year apart had been my way of finding something, the way she did in leaving things unfinished and never to be framed. Life wasn't a statement, just a few lines between pages and pages of notes and drawings. But again I failed to catch the mood, the hope of a homecoming; no matter what I wrote, the year as I described it sounded most clearly as a kind of failure. I hadn't managed to do anything on my own. None of it was real yet. I hadn't accepted that Anthony was gone and always would be gone.

I walked to the History Museum, read about rune stones and swords, and then left at closing time with aching legs and a mind filled with Viking commemorations, boasts, family trees. Outside, the rest of the world moved more quickly from finishing work to dinner. I threw away the letter, and crossed the bridge into the old part of town and trailed the last of the tourists as they cast their shadows against souvenir shops closing for the day. By seven, the wind numbed the back of my legs. I settled on an Italian restaurant I couldn't afford. I scanned the menu and calculated that I could manage a small margherita pizza and two glasses of red wine. It was still five hours until my next train, a night service to Trondheim, left.

The Italian waiters were kind-hearted and aloof. They seemed to sense it when someone needed to waste an evening, and left me to sit on my own against a back wall decorated with pictures of Portofino. Without thinking, I began a sketch of Claire. I didn't often draw, but now I was reproducing the way she'd stood in my room at Lion's Head, with her right arm over her head, held there with her left hand. Her face was turned away, turned into the arm. Her thick hair, the musculature of her arms, and her ribs raised against her torso – it was Claire of lines and distance. When I drew her like that, I liked the classical pose, and saw that it suited her. A pose like that could be unfinished, just as her sketches were.

At nine, I walked back towards the train station, and tried to organise the remaining hours into tasks and activities – find the platform, perhaps a coffee, read and finish the notes that I'd started earlier in the day – but I knew that I was in for a wait of cold boredom. I didn't think about either Anthony or Claire, but only the promise of sleep after I was allowed to board at eleven-thirty.

I woke in the upper bunk of the sleeper at eight. I had slept without moving, a dreamless night. I could remember getting on board, but not falling asleep, nor the train leaving the station. I was completely alone in a six-berth cabin: other passengers might have come and gone, but I had no memory of them, either.

My eyes adjusted to the faint light inside, and I lay still, waiting. An outline of silver bordered the curtains of the cabin window. I reached across from my bunk and drew the curtain towards me. The light inside barely changed: all that happened was that the faintness inside became part of a longer view that moved out. I stepped down to the lower bunk and sat facing the view. We'd entered the last valleys as they reached down to the fjords. A thick frost had settled over the farms and home fields, but also into the light on the conifers: the light was as white as snow.

And that's how that morning remains with me: the impossible perfection of the light that merged inside to out; the disappearance and dissolution the movement seemed to contain. And, strangely, how at the same time it insisted on the soul – the sense that at any moment the world could be illuminated for the singular observer, for us on our own. I was twelve again, young enough to swim and search for my mother, still unknowing in the way that mattered. I was in hospital, watching the light on the wooden window frame.

168

I was talking to Claire that afternoon shortly after we'd first met, when she asked if I felt my mother was still with us.

As we reached the fjords, the light yellowed. In my journal, I worried that it was all delusion, an echo of what I'd lost, a search for beauty. But behind the caution remained the more urgent feeling, about how we found the ones we love, even after they seemed to be gone. Was it absurd and sentimental, I wrote, to think that the answer lay in the light?

I wrote down the answer that came to me, as we pulled into Trondheim. I'd left Anthony for my own sake, when I should have stayed for him. The horrible truth was that I'd needed to be clear of him, of the responsibility of his love. And now I felt him coming back, in the light between the window and the world outside. What surprised me most was that I welcomed him.

24

I fell out of the Scandinavian autumn into a Sydney spring, and into all the openness and abundance of the harbour when it starts to warm. Dad met me at the airport. He stood in a brown jacket, reading the newspaper. He didn't people-watch, not even at the airport, and he tended to look uncomfortable in a crowd, for others noticed him. But seeing him there, before he saw me, I felt such pride in his good looks and self-possession. You sensed he could have stood there all day, holding a place in the world as long as it allowed him to stand still and read.

We went by taxi to Glebe Point Road. 'Can you bear it?' he asked.

'Yes.'

'I think it'd be a good idea for you to be here in Glebe today. Otherwise, it'll get bigger and bigger and you won't want to come back.'

A city of total openness, and yet a couple of suburbs back from the harbour also a city crumbling. Dad's favourite hotel was betraying its age. In the years since we'd first come to Sydney together, the rooms hadn't changed at all. They got older, that's all; the paint faded wherever people usually rested their hands, dropped their bags.

I switched on a light and the room revealed its tiredness, and then seemingly my own. And just as suddenly, when Dad left me to sleep off the flight, I was back in Anthony's place and knocking over the furniture to get to him. Lifting his hands from the sheets, crying because life and death were real. And the half-step of a foreign clock said: *Sleep. You're jetlagged.* Told me to let it disappear in the time difference and face it better when I woke up on Sydney time.

But the room revealed normality, too. In the time it took to unpack a bag, the world I thought I'd left forever, that couldn't be reclaimed, was familiar. I was inside it again. The body didn't forget the habits that had once constituted its place in Sydney, and the mind gradually caught up. I spent the morning in a coffee shop writing – I would keep going with the journal now that I'd started one. And then I walked to the university library, suspended above a future that my father was negotiating on my behalf. I took up a desk, loaded it with books on international law, and for the sake of familiarity resumed the persona of a student. Perhaps I'd leave for Denmark again.

It was a pretence that could last only so long. During our dinners, Dad said he'd mentioned me to people that he'd met with during the day. I was reminded again of how fondly others viewed him – how they wanted him in their lives. As in Lion's Head, they crowded around him at the first chance he gave to let them help.

In the end, I was offered a clerkship at a commercial firm that occupied two floors of a building on George Street. I knew what it meant. I would accept the favour, and spend the next thirty years accumulating the wealth I'd once promised to spend on Anthony and Claire. I didn't need the money anymore, but I accepted the job just as happily as if I did. I'd be busy; that was important. And I accepted my father's advice: he said you regained your confidence through work, if never entirely your old self. What had Jens said? Not everyone got the tap on the shoulder. Not everyone sacrificed themselves for a cause, because not everybody's sacrifice was needed.

It was sorted in a week. By the end of that period of worldly excitement, and with Dad gone home, I wanted only to know where Claire was. Though I had no real thoughts of contacting her. Or, rather, I'd come back with strong ideas about not contacting her. I didn't want to know how she was; that was something I couldn't hear yet. Perhaps she'd be with someone else by now. I didn't look up any of my friends, either. But I expected to run into them one day, and maybe they would tell me that Claire was married. One day she would figure that life went on in one form or another, and that in one form or another you eventually gave someone your remaining self. It would be her acquiescence, just as a job in commercial law was mine.

Every afternoon it was the same: I left the office and caught the bus to my new share-house in Newtown, past the house where she had lived. Until one night, I rang Dad to ask if he knew where she was living.

'Has she moved back to Sydney?' he said.

'What do you mean?'

'Well, she's been on the farm since you left. Didn't you know that?'

'No. We didn't write while I was away.'

'Then she's still there.' I was going to hang up, but Dad kept me. 'Anyway, I'm glad you rang. Anthony's father has been in touch. He says there are some paintings – a bundle of them – that Anthony left for you.'

'For me?'

'Well, I don't know. Possibly Claire, too. He didn't want to speak for long, and nor did I. He's going to drop them around.'

'I'll come up on the weekend,' I said.

'And Ted ...'

'Yes?'

'There's something else to talk about.'

'What is it?' I asked. 'Is everything alright?'

'We'll talk about it when you're here.'

'Can I bring Claire? If she'll come.'

I decided not to call her first. I thought it would make us both more nervous to have our reunion announced ahead. I caught the train to Lion's Head, and borrowed Dad's car for the drive to the farm. The road left the coast: the first rise followed around to the back of a range that blocked the views down to the sea, and replaced them with a scrub face punctuated by narrow driveways. When you came down on the other side it was all valleys tipping into creek beds, a landscape that gradually slumped into its trickle of brown water and blocks of silver reflection. Most of the farms in the area were still used for cattle, but here and there were orchards like the ones Claire's parents had started.

Another hour passed, and the road narrowed to a single-lane track. After two or three kilometres along it I felt lost, or rather I felt so far from the sea that the road seemed to be performing a kind of disappearance. On both sides, small tracks returned deeper into the bush, and I would've got lost if I had to find a side road. But the track ended at Claire's farm, and with the thought that I didn't know anything about how Claire had filled in the months between Anthony's death and that late afternoon. It was almost exactly a year.

And then – my first sight of her told me that she had been

waiting, here, since I left. She walked around the side of the farm-house just as I spoke to her father, who had let me go after a tight hug. She ran to me, and with her I felt again the complete, enclosed world of a wave. For the body remembered it, and how she tied me to the world.

'You're here,' she said. 'Don't go away again. Now you're back.'

25

'Come inside, Ted,' said Nikolas. 'You'll stay?'

'Yes. I mean, I'll check with Dad. I've got his car.'

'You should have brought him, as well,' he said. 'We've seen a lot of him the past year. We know about Copenhagen and your adventures with Jens.'

'From Dad?'

Claire turned to her father. 'Dad's been helping him with his vegetable garden. We think it's finally getting there. Oh, and the beach wall.'

'He didn't tell me,' I said.

'You were busy with your studies,' said Nikolas.

'I mean, he didn't tell me after I got back.'

As we walked inside, Claire asked, 'How long have you been home?'

'A few weeks,' I said. 'I'm sorry it's taken this long to come up. I wasn't sure if you wanted to see me.'

I rang Dad to tell him I was spending the night at the farm. Christina put me in the spare room, and for an hour after dinner I lay awake, hopeful that Claire might visit. She didn't come, and the following morning we drove back along the long dirt road down to the highway and out to Lion's Head.

'It's good to see the ocean,' said Claire. 'I want to go for a swim later. I haven't been out of the valley for a few weeks.'

'And you haven't been back to Sydney?'

'No, Dad went to get my things for me. I'm not sure I ever want to go back.'

'That might change,' I answered. We were going north along the highway, and as always the traffic in the opposite direction was thicker. It was like driving beside a stationary train that was heading the other way. 'Your work might take you there.'

'I like life on the farm. I didn't realise how much I'd missed it until I went back. I mean, went back properly – for longer than just a visit.'

'What about your painting?'

'I'm not too worried about that anymore. I prefer this.' She was gazing at the view, opening across to Lion's Head and the water.

'But drawing is what you do.'

'No,' she replied. 'You're wrong. I don't care if I never paint again.'

When we got to the house, Dad brought out the paintings – there was a bundle and a roll of them – and set them on the floor of my old bedroom. He left us to go through them together. I wondered whether Anthony had imagined how Claire and I would open the roll like this, sitting on the end of the bed where I once watched these paintings come to life. If so, I wanted to tell him that his death had created two ghosts, one for each of us to look out for, separately.

The paintings, it was obvious, hadn't been disturbed since his death. I undid the bundle, and as quickly felt like the witness again – for the conversation was between Anthony and Claire. I waited to see if she would leave. She was crying. I put the bundle back on the floor, and spread open the roll. The bigger pictures were familiar: self-portraits and paintings of Claire. But what caught our attention first was a smaller roll that slid out of the larger one. It was bound separately by its own piece of string.

The sheets were thick – watercolour paper that Anthony had used for pen and pencil sketches. In the top drawing, he'd traced the subjects in pencil, and then gone over the outlines in dark ink, a technique that created a sense of the figures in relief, and one that Claire had often used.

'He's copied your style in these,' I said.

'That's because it's us,' she replied.

I hadn't seen it. The first drawing could have been of any two people sitting next to one another, talking. But as we leafed slowly through the others, I saw that she was right. They were sketches that Anthony had made of Claire and me at those times when he'd sat a little apart from us in order to draw on his own.

'What is he saying with these?' I asked myself aloud.

'He isn't saying anything,' Claire said. 'That's why they're so lovely.'

Half or so had been drawn at Lion's Head – on the beach at the front of our house – but the last ones were all done in Sydney. There was a sketch of Claire sitting on a bench outside the state gallery; you could make out the main building and a sweep of driveway to the side. And another was of the two of us surrounded by the eclectic shrubbery of the botanic gardens.

I smiled. 'You'll like them because they're so like yours.'

'Probably,' she said. 'And I like them because it shows what he noticed about us. I used to think he never saw us properly. It wasn't his fault. He was too caught up in everything else.'

'Maybe that's why he left these. To show us.'

'I don't know,' she replied. 'I don't want to know why he left them.'

We walked down to the beach. 'Are you still afraid of swimming?' she asked.

'Probably. It's so long since I've tried, I'm not sure.'

'Would you mind if I went in?'

She stood at the end of a beach towel and unwrapped her skirt. She was wearing a yellow bikini. She stood with her hands on her waist, her stomach pressed out a little. I remembered undressing her, the car lights. Lifting her shirt over raised arms.

'You didn't think you could write to me?' I said.

'Not yet. You left, remember.'

She knelt down and folded her clothes on the towel. Her face was close. 'Come in with me,' she said. 'The water looks beautiful.'

'I'd rather wait for you here.' I was watching her in her bikini.

'Do you like it?' she asked.

'I like you in it. It's very yellow.'

She walked slowly to the shoreline, almost on her toes. Was that how she usually walked on sand? I couldn't remember. She was straightening her legs for me. When the water reached her waist, she raised her hands and called out, 'It's lovely!'

'I love you,' I called back.

Then she dived in. Into the split world of water and sky, while I watched and waited for her to come back.

'You should've come in,' she said after, a little breathless, as she rested on her elbows. I was lying with my head on my arm. The salt water dripped from her face onto mine. I held her hand again, but in a fraction of a moment she drew back. 'I'm sorry.'

What for, I wondered? For pulling away, or for me and the mistake I'd made? I said, 'I don't blame you if you don't want to see me. You don't owe me anything.'

'I never thought I owed you anything.' She still wore an open expression. 'Do you think you could stop offering to leave me?' I wanted to kiss her, reach for her hand again. As if she sensed it, she sat up. 'The water's beautiful,' she repeated.

'It's not the water,' I snapped. 'I don't need you to tell me what the water's like.'

'No.'

Claire waited for me to explain; I was thinking about how quickly and quietly she'd moved away. Then she stood. 'I'm going home. Will your dad drive me?'

She started up the dune. 'Don't come now,' she said. For the first time I could remember, I heard sarcasm in her voice. 'Phone me when you get back to Sydney. Phone me and tell me how much you care.'

26

Dad held his hands together. I noticed the patience that was in them, and remembered how I'd once fancied that they showed the fishing boats coming into Whitby at the end of the day; the way that generation after generation had waited for the right weather, for news of those at sea, for prices and economies that never got any better. These were things he'd prepared me for on the few occasions we sat together and talked about Whitby, and the times we talked about my mother. During those boyhood conversations, I felt the sheets of coastal rain; the endless opera weather, as he later came to call it. The smell of wet tobacco. The water's edge, and a photograph taken of us, with my mother's arm around my waist. All this seemed contained by his hands and the way, sometimes, that he'd rub them together and release the dust of all those secret places.

He rubbed them now, and said that he didn't find any injustice in it. I believed him, because I knew what he was waiting for – to be with Mum in Whitby. Consciousness would go, and the fence posts would fall into the sea, whether you wanted it or not.

He said, 'I've so seldom been unwell. I don't know how to be a patient.'

'You've never feared death.'

'No,' he replied, 'or not so much my own.'

It was perhaps an unnecessary thing to say to a son, and I doubt he would have wanted anyone else to hear it. But it was also merely one more test in a suite of exams that I'd long been sitting on the subject of what he might really be saying. His private self was there, a faint variation that played alongside the main theme, a cadence for which I'd long since trained my ear. It was always there, even within the broad Yorkshire musicality that had left me with an in-between accent and given him such a steady, filling presence in his own theatre, the local courtroom.

He showed me the x-rays as dispassionately as a piece of evidence. 'You do realise this is you?' I said. 'This isn't someone else.'

'This is an x-ray,' he said. 'That's what I realise.'

'Examining your body.'

He tried to make light of it. 'I've never been my best in photographs.' He waited for a reaction, but when I didn't bite he added, 'Did you ever notice that photographs aren't the least bit realistic? They exaggerate certain features over others. Look at me. Right now, I tell you, I am fine.'

He did seem well, perhaps even better than usual. Something shone in him. 'How old are you, Dad?'

'Now you ask me!'

'Are you fifty?'

'Thereabouts,' he answered. He put his hand gently on the back of my neck and drew me close. 'Come out to the garden.'

He'd come to treat the vegetable patch as though it were a council allotment, a place of refuge for the inner Yorkshireman. Gardening kept him brown and fit, but more than that it kept at bay a passive outlook that you saw in his friends, except perhaps Eric. Dad spoke to his plants now, seemingly treating them as the ultimate witnesses and conspirators of his resilience. I supposed Nikolas had taught him that while I was away – how to use his vegetable garden properly, as a sort of companion. But however fit he seemed, I could also tell that he'd started waiting.

'What do you want to do?' I asked.

'I want to go back,' he said. 'And I want you to come with me. I want you to come with me to Whitby. It's time we went.' I think I must have sighed. 'What is it?'

'Nothing.' And then I struggled to catch something of what was finally granted. In a way, it was too perfect to catch. 'I want to go to Whitby, Dad. I've wanted it for a long time.'

'I know. We'll go and find something for both of us.'

When I got back to Sydney, I decided to follow Claire's instructions, however angrily they'd been given. I phoned her. I wanted to tell her that I was about to put in my notice at the law firm. That I'd stay in Sydney until June or July, and then Dad and I would go back to Whitby for a holiday together.

'Is that why you're calling, Ted?'

'Dad's unwell,' I said.

'Is he going to be alright?'

'I don't know. He doesn't want to take it seriously. He doesn't really believe the doctors, even though he says he does.'

'You should come back, then.'

'He doesn't want the fuss. He wants me to stay in Sydney.'

'I'd like to see you.'

'I thought you might want to come to Sydney,' I suggested. 'Have a week here. There's a spare room at my place.'

'Who do you share with?'

'Other lawyers.'

'No, you come here.'

So the next time I visited Dad, I went one day to see Claire at the farm, and found her again as her ancestral self. She was collecting up bits and pieces from around the farm – a stool that her grandmother had given her once in Corfu; pots and pans that her mother wanted to replace and would've thrown out.

'Why are you getting all those things?' I asked.

'They're for your place. For you and the lawyers to share.'

'Will you come for a visit?'

'I don't know. You've cut your hair?' she said.

'Oh, my hairdresser told me I needed a change.'

'Do you always do what your hairdresser tells you?'

'Yes.'

'Maybe I should start cutting your hair then.'

'What would you do?' I asked.

'I'd shave it all off and start again.' Claire put her hand in my hair, and then shook it. 'Or maybe just mess it up a bit. It's too tidy for you.'

'Well, I'm a lawyer now.'

'You should quit.'

'Be a ship builder or writer,' I agreed. 'Eric might need me. Otherwise, I'm going to write books.'

'I wish you would.'

'Don't tell Eric. He'd be heartbroken.'

After lunch, I asked her again if she'd thought about the trip to visit me.

'No, I'm not coming to Sydney. But take these things from the farm,' she said. 'What do you think?'

I wasn't sure that Claire's mother quite understood what Claire was doing with her old things. I asked Claire if she'd told her about the disappearing household.

'No.' She checked, and saw me smile. 'Well, she'd be horrified if I said that all of her old things were being used at your place. She thinks you're such a fancy-pants.'

'Fancy-pants?'

'See. I can't even use words like that around you.'

Perhaps Christina was right. But surely I should have been wary of decorating my new place with a very brown set of serving bowls, straight out of the seventies, that were now being placed in the backseat of Dad's car. Claire was sure I could adapt them for the city. She filled the bowls with oranges and tomatoes.

'Don't drive too fast later,' she said. 'The tomatoes will fall out.'

'Okay.'

'Is there anything else you need?'

'I'd love one or two of your drawings.'

We went to a spare room at the back of the house. It looked like her pictures hadn't been moved since she'd come back from art college. A roll of them leant against a column of shoeboxes in a back cupboard. That afternoon we leafed through her folios together.

Claire showed me a series of nude studies, of the art college models. And then a lover's necessary next step, to turn the question back on himself: 'Have you ever drawn me?'

'Not yet.'

Behind the nudes were the drawings I liked most of all, her early studies of Lion's Head. In one was the Head, drawn from the other side, the rougher bay. Caught at that time of day when the lower rocks of the Head were orange and the low trees cast long shadows across the cliffs at the end.

'You got it on a calm day,' I said.

'That side is prettier,' she replied.

'Did Anthony ever draw the rocks?'

'Normally he just watched me. You know, he didn't think he could paint landscapes.'

'Not like you,' I said. 'He meant he couldn't paint landscapes like you can.'

'Stop,' she said. 'Let's stop.'

I drove from the farm back to Lion's Head, and rather than take her gifts to Sydney I left them in the house – the brown bowls, the stool and two drawings of Lion's Head.

27

More regularly now, Dad was needed at the hospital for treatment and further tests. I organised a break from work, and once again took the train home. Ostensibly, I was there to see that Dad had all he needed, but I seemed to be also there to witness a change in him. Bitterness had finally replaced the bleak humour over the x-rays that had come home from the clinic in town.

But he was right. They weren't exactly photographs. They were charts and directions, and now he had no choice but to follow their course with his hands – from inside the x-rays to the surface of his chest. He touched it involuntarily. Gradually, inside the latest images the white moved further across. It was smoke. The cigars had crept into the walls.

That night, I dreamt that the white shadow had worked its way into his throat. In the dream, we were checking the x-rays together. I held one, but he snatched it from me and threw it to the ground, and said, 'Yes, alright, now it looks like me.'

One morning, a letter arrived from England. I brought it to him in his study.

'It's from Lillie,' my father said when I handed him the envelope. 'Your aunt.'

'I thought so. She's still got your handwriting.'

He read the letter and folded it back into the envelope. 'She's unwell. She wants to know if we'll visit.'

'Can I read it?'

He held it in the fisherman's net of his hands, and then stood up to put it next to his cigar box, hidden in a small cupboard in the corner of the room.

'Later.' He looked up. 'Smoke?' When I declined, he said, 'We owe her a visit.'

It was time to return the visit she'd made in that last summer before Anthony and Claire left for Sydney, when Anthony was staying with us at Lion's Head, and Claire came over most days, too, together planning the ultimate escape to Sydney.

I stood beside Dad and looked at the letter and the cigar box. 'Do you want to smoke?' I asked.

'Yes, let's go outside.'

As we walked, I said we'd visit Lillie together.

'Have you got my cigar?' he asked as we crossed the road. 'Light it for me. My hands shake.'

There was every chance we'd still make it back. 'I'd like it if we both went to Whitby.'

'Yes, I want to visit Lillie with you. But I wouldn't stay in Whitby,' he answered. 'I'd want to be based in Durham.' Where he went to university, where he and my mother had met.

'It'll make for long days,' I said. 'The drive to Whitby is too long, I think.'

'You drive, I'll sleep.'

I took this as a yes. The next day, I began to make enquiries for our trip. We'd do as he wished and stay in Durham, but we would also return to Whitby.

But the following morning, Dad called off any arrangements I was making. 'I'll write to Lillie,' he said, 'tell her what the doctors have told me. I'm not well enough.'

'Let's go to Whitby now. Before it gets worse.'

'There's no time.'

'It takes a day to fly to England.'

'There's no time,' he insisted.

'Dad, I'm never going to make a good lawyer.'

'I know. Don't worry about that. Do something you want.'

'I mean, I have time. I don't need to be in Sydney. I'll finish up at the firm early.'

'No,' he said, 'I've made up my mind. I'm not going back, not like this. It's too late.'

He tried to give up cigars. But the withdrawals were too severe. He told me that they left him breathless. Without cigars as a conciliatory addiction he retreated into silence even before the illness forced it, muted not so much by closeness to death but by how quiet the world seemed at those times when he would usually smoke and listen to music.

I bought him an iPod, and his doctor said the breathless feeling would pass. It might have, had he kept trying. But to the nurses' dismay, a miserable week after he tried to stop he began to smoke again, and perhaps even more heavily than before. He made an effort to conceal it, but I could tell by the way he returned to his old self.

I stayed on in Lion's Head, and began to phone Claire every day. To my surprise, I found that she wanted a part in reprimanding me, a task that the nurses seemed also to take pleasure in. First, it was about the cigars. In our phone conversations she told me that I shouldn't help him smoke.

'Since when have you been so strict?' I said.

'Since I got to know him,' Claire replied, 'while you were in Denmark. I want him to get better.'

And then she disapproved of persuading my father to go to Whitby. In this, she was entirely on Dad's side. Why press him to travel to England if he was happy here? 'Maybe the illness has shown him what matters. He wants to be with the people he loves.'

'But I'm the only person he loves,' I said.

'I think he loves me more than you these days,' she joked.

She might have been right, but still I tried to convince him. If there was a break in the treatment, we'd make a short visit – it need only take a week or two.

'I'll even let you pay,' I told him.

We drove to Nambucca Heads for a break from the house and Lion's Head. For a while, we sat by the estuary wall. It was cold. I wrapped him in a blanket and we turned our backs to the sea. He smoked, but at long last he wasn't enjoying it. Because I was so often lighting his cigars, I'd found a taste for them. Halfway through, he gave me his cigar and I finished it for him.

'You got my note?' he asked.

'Yes, I got it.'

On my desk, he'd left a strangely formal letter telling me that he wanted to be interred in town, at the local cemetery. He began by assuring me that he wasn't meaning to be officious, that he wouldn't normally think to put this kind of thing in writing. But he was worried. It said, *I know you hoped for us to go back. But I'm quite at peace with ending my days here.*

I wasn't thinking that far ahead. All the same, I asked whether he wasn't making a mistake. If it came to that, wouldn't he like his ashes taken to Whitby?

'Please follow my wishes,' he said, summoning all that was left of the judge's voice. 'You have them now, in advance. I've expressed it very clearly. And I'm sure it's the right thing. If you don't follow a wish of that kind, you're telling me that my final moments are yours to decide.'

'It's okay, I'll do what you tell me,' I replied. But it struck me as such a bitter thing to want, this punishing of his soul by confining it to a country to which he'd never really belonged. 'You don't feel at home here,' I said. 'I always thought you'd want to be buried with Mum.' Why else had he saved himself?

'It's not up to you.' He rushed the words out, as though he'd been waiting to say them for some time. I still had my arm over his shoulder, holding the blanket in place. I held him closer. I wanted to lighten the conversation, but I couldn't find another topic.

'Ted, I want to stay here. If I were meant to go back, we would've made it by now. Lillie understands.'

'Has she written again?'

He put his hand up to mine, gripped it on the edge of the blanket. It was a loving gesture, I thought. But it was also the gesture of a father who didn't think he was getting through to his son. 'Tell me again that you really want to be buried here,' I said.

'Let's walk. You're getting morbid.' He stood up and said hello to a friend, who wanted our bench.

'Are we all out today?' the man asked.

'You'll need a blanket,' said my father, and gave him ours.

190

We took a footpath that followed the Nambucca River as the estuary widened out to the heads. On a retaining wall of large boulders was painted an informal exhibition of pictures by families who'd visited for holidays, seemingly always to this same spot on the mid-coast of New South Wales. The paintings comprised lists of family members and the years they'd come. Some also contained pretty, naive portraits, often drawn by the children.

In one, the parents stood on either side of the family dog, with brothers and sisters grouped together and the family framed by the red and yellow flags of the lifesavers. In another, the dream of perfect symmetry was replaced by a floating affinity: the family was represented as a seahorse surrounded by circles, perhaps eggs, each named after a family member.

There were memorials, too. There was one that upset my father. It was for a boy who'd died in 1999, aged one. The memorial read: *In our thoughts you are happy in His kingdom, in our hearts you are with us every day, in our arms you are sadly missed.* Underneath the inscription were stick people drawn by his siblings.

'They must be young adults now,' I said.

My father said, 'You find out that you'll accept whatever time there is.'

'I love you, Dad,' I said.

'I'm frightened. I'm surprised to find I'm frightened.'

The afternoon fishermen were out. The light over the estuary was sandy, but the ocean was pale grey. Seagulls gathered on a sand island that lay between us and the next headland; they seemed painted into stillness there – broken lines of musical notation. On the other side of the island, the beach began again and ran without pause to Lion's Head.

I wasn't giving up quite yet. I asked whether walking along the wall, especially in the cool evenings, ever reminded him of home.

'The fish smell's the same,' he replied, 'but no coal. No smoke.'

'Will you write to Lillie?'

'I have. I've told her we won't come. She knows why. She knows I want to stay.' He was breathless as we walked. He put his hand on my shoulder.

The pressure of that hand seemed to stay on my shoulder that evening, when I sat on my own in the house, in the repetition of a phrase, a command from my childhood. *Listen to it. Carefully.* Sometimes said almost desperately, speaking in the instant of Puccini or Ravel or Verdi or whichever of the great composers we'd reached, but only ever instructing me in the matter of the voice, and what it meant to recognise the truth in the voice of another.

He'd married a religious woman, and so, he claimed, he didn't need God. But he'd found God in sounded words – and I supposed in hers more than any others. His sense of the greater truth of things had found its best moments in music, the artform he trusted: whoever you were, he said, would come out in the voice.

I thought I could hear it now, a melodic line that rose alongside or deeper inside his stated wishes – a question about himself and my mother that he hadn't been able to answer in Australia. He didn't want to go back to Whitby. But something was waiting for us there.

28

My father's last love was the Russian soprano Anna Netrebko. The morning after we walked along the estuary wall at Nambucca Heads, he put on one of her recitals. He was showing off a set of new speakers, and had the volume up. He chose 'Qui la voce sua soave' – 'Here, his sweet voice' – from Bellini's last opera, *I Puritani*. It ended with the imploration, 'Give me back hope or let me die'. In the moment it was his pathos and autobiography, neither of which he would usually think good reasons for listening to music, or proper points of encounter. He thought the meaning of music lay behind these things, behind the threshold of direct appeals.

But after he played it, he said, 'Did you listen to me yesterday?'

'Yes,' I replied, 'I did.'

'Good. Because I've told you what I want.'

And yet, as though in the sleeve of the record, there was still something else – a second request, from my mother, that his voice seemed also to carry. The photograph, and how it had for so long stayed in my father's desk drawer. I had the strongest feeling that he wanted to put it back. But I couldn't.

*

We were waiting for Claire to arrive. We talked about the weeks ahead, and what the doctors were telling him. He said he wanted to stay at home, not go up to the hospital, even if the illness got worse. He was feeling well enough to take care of himself.

I suspected he didn't want to leave his record collection, or his cigars. 'You should stay at home, then,' I said. 'I'm sure you'll feel better here.'

Claire had finally agreed to visit me in Sydney. She stayed at Dad's place overnight, and he said I could take his car instead of catching the train; he wasn't using it. Early the next day, while it was still dark, we stepped into a windy darkness, with sand in the air, and lit up the bends as we wound towards the highway. It was too early to talk. I thought Claire might be sleeping, but when I stopped for fuel she jumped out and said she'd do it. 'I feel like a stretch. Do you want a coffee?'

'I'll get the coffees, you do the fuel,' I answered.

When we were back on the road, Claire said, 'Your dad wants me to go over the arrangements for the funeral.'

'What's happened?'

'Nothing. It's not that.' She took my coffee to hold. 'Last night after you went to bed he said there were things he wanted to go over. He thinks you won't follow his instructions.'

'He said that?'

'He thinks you've decided to take his ashes to Whitby.'

'We'd talked about going back. He wanted to. That's why it's come up.'

'I told him you wouldn't do anything he didn't ask.'

'Right.'

I wasn't sure what to say next, but something held me back from giving her the promise she wanted – assuring her that I would follow his wishes. She waited for a response. But the further we drove the less sure I was.

By the time we reached Sydney the drive had turned into a very long one to Central Station. She was going to get the next service back. It was a mistake to come to Sydney like this.

'I don't want you to go back to the farm. Stay a few days.'

Again, she waited for the promise that I wouldn't ever take his ashes to Whitby. I didn't say anything.

'I don't want to be part of this,' she said. We were stopped outside the station. 'I just can't.'

'I'm not asking you to go to Whitby,' I shouted.

She opened the car door. 'You don't yell at me,' she said. She stepped out and slammed the door. 'Don't yell at me,' she repeated, and walked up to the station.

The phone call came at work, during a meeting. I answered my phone in front of the others in the office. It was Dad's GP. My father had been taken to hospital. Most probably a heart attack. I replied I was four or five hours' drive away. Would I be there in time? The doctor hesitated. He wasn't sure; he wasn't with Dad at the moment.

He said to get to the hospital. That was the main thing now.

He's dead. Was that what the GP wanted to say? I wanted to reply, *Stop him then. Call him back.*

I drove and my chest ached – a strange pain, a burning that replaces the warmth that the body has known. The knowledge was there, in that heat, located as a kind of despairing certainty. But also as impossibility – he had died, but that couldn't be. I drove through the high rock walls that had been carved out for the highway, and there again a wave of knowledge that he was gone, before we could really say anything. Before I could tell him for certain that I'd listened. That I knew there was more to his story and Mum's.

I phoned ahead, and demanded to know. I upset the nurse who answered. Yes, he'd died shortly after arriving. They'd been trying to reach me on my mobile.

I hadn't heard the phone. 'Did he say anything?' I asked.

'I'm sorry, no.' A silence. Then, 'You should come in. I'll put the doctor on.'

'Are you driving?' the doctor said when he picked up.

'Yes.'

'You should pull over.'

'Okay, I will,' I said. 'Is he dead?'

'Your father died when he got to the hospital. Can you come in?'

I pulled off the freeway. I was shaking. I put the phone down and picked it back up.

'Can you come in?' the doctor asked again.

'Yes, I'm coming,' I answered at last.

When I got there, I was shown into a room that hummed cold, a room of steel furniture and white panels where he lay.

And then I drove to the house. Only as I pulled into the lane did I realise I was home. I went inside quickly, to check on things, even if there was no reason to.

There were no signs of a fall. There was only the sense that the furniture had been moved and tidied. By Eric, I thought. A cigar box beside the speaker. I opened it and closed it. And next to the cigar box, the letter from Lillie that Dad had said I could read later.

18 May

My dear brother,

I wonder whether you will think it strange of me to write after all this time. It's not so much for my own sake, but because I think you would want to know. We have had our fights, but I am sure you would be angry with me if I didn't tell you that I was unwell and that there isn't much time left. My doctor knows that I have a brother in Australia. He suggested I write to you now.

I have asked you to come before, when you drove me to the airport to catch the flight home. I believed then, as I do now, that there are some things that can only be mended by you coming home. And by that I want to say that I still believe something can be mended. It isn't too late, because I know you still love her and always did love her.

Bring Ted. Show him where you and Isabel lived and where he was born. Let me see the two of you again.

I am still at the old house. I don't reply when they write to move me. The nearest place that will have me is Doncaster. I won't go. I have decided to live out my days here, by the sea. Like you, Theodore. So they've given me some care. Angela is a sort of nurse who calls in two or three times each week. Apart from that, I'm alone with my thoughts. Often, I wish I would lose my mind, like some of my friends have.

You will remember what you said, that you would come back if I asked you to. Write back now and tell me that you'll be here soon.

Your loving sister,

Lillie

'He can't,' I said out loud.

I wanted him with me, the man I'd followed as he trailed cigar smoke, knowing that I breathed it in.

29

The funeral was held on a cold, blue day in June. The chapel was lined on either wall with sliding glass doors that seemed closed off by the throng of people who couldn't fit inside. The sun came in over their heads, and lit the front row with the full brightness of a winter afternoon. My father lay before us, his face quieted.

I thought about Dad and Anthony, and the conversations they'd had when Anthony had stayed with us – about the law and the possibility of change. Mostly, the people there knew my father as a lawyer, and in the main that's how I felt he should be remembered. I explained to the congregation that I'd thought I was going to be a diplomat – and that was why I'd once become interested in the UN and spent a year studying in Copenhagen with students much brighter than I was.

'When I told this to my father, though, he replied that diplomacy was still an artform practised almost exclusively by the privileged. He wasn't sure it would suit the grandson of a Yorkshire fisherman. He thought salt water and fish scales were harder to clean off than that.'

There was a murmur of appreciation. I went on, 'In his study at home, my father built his own wooden bookshelves when we first moved here nearly twenty years ago. Upon them, Dad collected three thousand books and a thousand records. He was a fisherman, yes, but in every sense the fisherman who'd come in from the sea, and was happy on land.'

I spoke a little longer, and then finished the eulogy with a quote from Dag Hammarskjöld, the man whose beliefs my father had shared:

> When the sense of the earth unites with the sense of one's body, one becomes earth of the earth, a plant among plants, an animal born from the soil and fertilising it.

Then I stood to the side of the coffin while the procession of mourners approached. For a moment, I rather resented them. But Claire had left out a wide bowl of frangipani petals for people to place beside him. I thought he would have liked that she'd put them there, and it changed the day and my vague sense of resentment, my hostility towards those who'd come that was really just my hostility to the fact that it was happening at all. I still wasn't able to look at him, and struggled to contain a feeling that others shouldn't, either. But after placing their flowers, many pressed a kiss on their fingers and then on his ash-grey temple, and then touched my hand or put their arms around me. I found I wanted them there, after all.

There was a dark comedy to the day, as I suppose there often is at funerals. Some spoke to him. People he didn't drink with promised to have a round in his honour. Those he'd unpicked from endless boundary disputes promised him a peaceful journey to the hereafter. Women he'd fled promised him that he was about to be reunited with his wife; he was a widower no longer. Miss Weston stood longer than most, but I didn't hear her speak.

Meanwhile, I tried to stand as still as I could, as though once again watching them pause in front of our house, looking along the line of posts from the beach to the road. A moment of good-willed gossip; an imploration to a lonely man to let go of the past and fall in love again, connect to a woman as a way of reconnecting to the world. I saw that their sadness today was that they had failed. Yes. For no matter where he was buried, he was on his way back, and I still believed in helping him there. He was still mine to help.

Claire caught my eye. She shook her head and smiled. It meant, *Don't listen*. She sat at the front row with Eric and her parents. As her mother's hand rested on her forearm, it seemed Claire's age had halved, entirely the young daughter again, the world contracted to those afternoons when we came back to Lion's Head and the days ended on the cusp of the dune, when we'd find each other's backs to lean against and each other's hands to hold.

I hadn't seen her since our argument in Sydney. Outside the chapel, her eyes were bright, but also stern, as they'd so often been since we first met – the girl at the hospital who wanted the stranger sorted out before she let him in. She stayed close to me during the wake, which was held at the funeral home.

'What are you going to do now?' she asked later, as we got into Dad's car together. That was her defence against the sadness of the day, just as it had been in the hospital when we first met.

'Do you mean, the ashes?'

'Yes.'

'I'm not sure,' I said. 'They said to collect them the next time I'm home.' Dad hadn't arranged a plot for the interment. Most of all, I wanted to let her know that I was glad she'd come to the funeral, and that I'd wanted her here for my sake, not just for Dad's.

'Can I put some music on?' I asked.

'Yes.'

I chose Bellini, and *I Puritani*, because it was the one opera that Claire liked as much as my father had; it was always at the top of the stack in the car.

'Did you know this opera was Queen Victoria's favourite?' she said.

'I'm sure Dad did. I hadn't realised he shared a favourite with her. I must admit I like the idea of them together in some way.'

'I looked it up on Wikipedia for you.'

'Are you starting to like opera?'

'Probably not. But I dislike it less when I know what's going on.'

Neither of us really knew what was going on. Still, we followed the overture as it took us out of the traffic. The curtain rose to the ocean, and to Pavarotti and Sutherland exchanging familiar blows: 'A te, o cara' – 'To you, dear one'.

'Do you know how to get through this?' she asked.

'I don't.'

'You're the same as your father.' I thought we were about to start fighting again, but her voice was conciliatory, faint. 'And you're still getting over what happened to Anthony.'

'I'm going to Whitby.'

'Wait a year,' she said. But I saw no reason to wait. She went on, 'You need some time before you decide what to do next.'

'I can't. Lillie's unwell.'

'Come to the farm for a bit.'

'Claire.'

She turned away. 'Alright, I'll stop.'

*

She stayed that night with me in Lion's Head, at the house. I gave her the spare room, while I had mine. For most of the evening we were like housemates. Claire cooked, as though it were her turn. I did the dishes, as though it were mine.

After dinner, I showed her a copy of deeds that lay among a collection of yellowed papers. Dad had brought them from England when we first moved. They showed that he and Lillie had been joint owners of a terrace house in Whitby, and that, upon Dad's death, Lillie owned the property in full. The other papers revealed that he had made regular payments to Lillie, it seemed both for her living costs and for the upkeep of the house.

In the days before the funeral, I'd phoned to tell her that Dad had died. I also wanted her to know that the contributions would continue, and that Dad had left money for this in the will. I offered to buy a plane ticket so that she could come to the funeral. She couldn't travel that far. Then I asked whether the amounts Dad had sent were enough to cover her costs. She answered yes, and that she'd write soon.

'She'll still be there in a year,' Claire said.

'Come with me now,' I asked.

'No. I don't want you to go to England right now.'

'Come with me,' I said again.

'No.'

In the morning, Claire's dad picked her up and she went back to the farm. I drove to Sydney. She called the next day, and asked whether I was eating properly. Then she offered to come to the city, but I said I was fine. I started the mornings with a croissant and an espresso at the museum, as a way of placing myself in the world, a table to the side and an open view of the morning. In Sydney, you smell the ocean; in the enclosure of tables you feel the shadow of the trees.

But while I sat in the company of strangers and commuters, my thoughts followed the paths that I'm sure Claire knew they would, to her and my father. Claire was leaving me; I could feel myself pushing her away, and part of me wanted to push harder, so that I wouldn't have to consider the happiness that might lie on the other side. I could be my father, if I wished, waiting in the study, watching the water.

On my last day at the firm, I followed the gardens down to Farm Cove. It had been one of the places Anthony would come when he needed to get away from art college. He'd stand at the water's edge. If you were standing on the shore, he said, then you were halfway there. To wherever you wanted to go. Tomorrow you could be in New York. Or Lion's Head.

The next morning, I headed out of Sydney. It was an awkward drive. I was out of sync with the traffic and the road, and misjudged the distance of the bends as they approached. It began to rain heavily, but the traffic didn't slow. My thoughts wandered constantly to Claire, as I listened to Bellini like we had on the drive from the funeral. Then I drove past the turnoff to Lion's Head to the funeral home and collected Dad's ashes.

I placed the urn on a bookshelf in Dad's study. A few minutes later, Eric arrived with a letter from Lillie, along with a collection of subscriptions: the Law Society newsletter, a *London Review of Books*, a new recording of *The Magic Flute*.

'Do I keep looking out for all this junk?' he asked.

'Yes. I don't think I'll cancel them.'

'I was surprised to see the car,' he said. 'I didn't know you'd be up so soon.'

'I might stay a while,' I replied. 'I've got a few things of Dad's to sort out. You don't need to send the mail to Sydney.'

'Alright.' He handed me more letters. 'Listen, can I borrow you this afternoon? Do you have time?'

'Yes.'

'I need help with the path. Do you have time?' he asked again, as though I possibly hadn't meant it.

'Of course I do.'

'Around two, then.'

Eric closed the door and left me with the letters. In Lillie's, she reminded me of the visit she'd made during my last year of school, and asked me if I'd visit her in Whitby. Her health was up and down. She wanted to know me again, she wrote, while there was time.

I remember, from my visit when you were sixteen, how much I loved the home that you and your father had made in Lion's Head. But I also thought he was terribly lonely, and I worried that his loneliness would one day be yours, because he seemed so determined not to come home. I don't know if he told you, but he and I fought badly that summer. And there has been such a silence between us ever since. I didn't think this was how you were, but I saw that you understood him, even at that age.

Still, you are much more like your mother. She always wanted things to be said aloud, fully.

Ted, your father's last letter told me about how you lost your friend Anthony, who I remember meeting. But you and Claire are still friends. I'd so like to hear about all of these things from you. We have so much to catch up on.

30

Eric had put out wood stained with creosote and cut into triangles, leant against trestles to dry. As we worked, the afternoon brought only thin winter light through gums braced by undergrowth. When, across the road, the canopy began to throw a distracted shadow towards the beach, Eric said we were about halfway. He passed me a bottle of water.

'I'll go up and get us a coffee,' I told him.

'Wait until we're finished,' he said. 'Another five or six steps and we'll reach the gate.'

He'd brought me in to help muscle a boulder out of the way. It was a short job, but I'd stayed and now we were having the afternoon together. If I wasn't careful, I'd soon be the new member of the great project to replace all the paths from the road up to the beach. We broke up another step and then installed the new planks. It took a few goes to find a pattern that worked and that we could repeat quickly: break up the old path and clear it away, set the frame, place the wooden planks and level them, fill them in, and then level again.

'I bumped into Diane today,' said Eric, 'from the funeral home.'

'Oh?'

'She said you'd collected the ashes.'

'Yes. Can I make that coffee now?'

'No, we've got another hour in us, at least.'

I was desperate not to offend Eric, but I was still unsure about what those ashes were asking from me. Had Claire also spoken to him? 'You probably know that he asked to be buried here.'

'Will you let me tell you something he once said? It was after your accident, while you were still in hospital.'

'Yes.'

'There wasn't any reason you'd notice this as a boy, but he was very low at that time. For a few days, they thought you might die. Did you know that? He blamed himself. He said he hadn't given you the care you needed; the whole thing was his fault.'

'I know all this.'

'Listen for a second.'

'Sorry. I'm listening.'

'Your dad told me that he'd have to try harder to put the past out of his mind. He thought you were so reckless because he wasn't close enough to you as a father. Do you see that?'

'We had our own ways of dealing with Mum's death. I understood that. I didn't ever blame him for it. The problem was that he never really gave her to me. He kept her to himself.'

'That was grief, Ted. He wanted to be more in your life.'

'He was ready to go back. He told me. There's something there he needed to go back for. I'm sure he wanted it.'

Eric took the shovel from me. 'You can't burn ashes. That's not how it works. That's when we get to rest.' He held the handle, and for a moment was going to try again. 'Have you spoken to Claire?' he asked.

'Yes,' I said.

'Talk to her again, then.' He leant the shovels against a post and concluded, 'Alright, make me a coffee.'

I booked myself on a flight to London that would leave in a week's time. Afterwards, I held his wooden cigar box, smelt it, and then I put it at the end of a line of records that concluded with *The Death of Klinghoffer*. Between them, enough Wagner to fill a Viking mound, enough Verdi to produce tears and irritation from the whole population of Lion's Head.

My hand rested on the corner of *I Puritani*, but I settled on *Norma*, the recording with Edita Gruberová. To open the windows and share the high notes, I thought, would be just the thing. If I played the music loudly enough, even Eric would hear that one note that I had heard, the one that said even the oldest questions could be answered. There was time.

Then, a week of late nights, waiting. I sat up drinking Dad's coffee and then wine and then scotch, and tried to write about the coming journey, but in fact wrote very little: nothing real would come until I'd left, I knew. And so the usual stimulants to writing took me instead to a stack of CDs and records, and a vague sorting process. I discovered that his collection was ordered by date of purchase, so I thought I might catalogue them as a timeline of his listening life. It seemed a way to order the week, as well – I'd do a decade per day. But each time I started, rather than finishing a section, I found a record I hadn't heard him play for a few years and put it on, and I began stealing his cigars, too.

The smoke and the music played a kind of dedication. And at the same time they supplied the injunction to write an email to Claire, for I knew that Eric was right: I had to explain better why I was going.

I know why you don't want me to go. At the end, Dad said he didn't want to, and I see, like you, that he was meaning to protect me, just as Anthony wanted to protect me when he sent me home that night. But the truth is, Claire, that night I knew it straight away, felt it. Underneath my anger at what was happening I knew that I shouldn't have left Anthony and shouldn't have gone home. I've learnt that you have to listen better than I did then.

I think Dad wanted to protect me, and maybe that's why you're upset with me. Because I won't take the warning. He wanted to protect me when I was a boy, and I didn't take the warning then, either. I know what you're thinking: look how that ended. Yes, but it also ended with me meeting Anthony and you, my two most precious friends. And so much more than that, as well.

I'm sure that Dad knows I am going back. I don't blame you if you're angry with me for this. But at least now you see my thoughts.

Your Ted

During the night I checked, but Claire didn't reply. I slept fitfully until three; not really believing that I'd slept, only that the time on the clock had changed. The wind was up, and I wasn't as used to the banging of the screens anymore – I moved from my old room to Dad's, because it was further back in the house and more sheltered from the weather. At five, the wind dropped completely and I got up wondering if it had been a good idea to write to Claire.

I walked down to the beach. I expected Eric to appear, but it was still too early, and for an hour I was alone on the dune. The salt air laid its second skin, its greasy insulation, and I didn't feel cold until the sun broke. Then, one of the sandbanks to the north was lifted out of the sea by strips of gold seaweed that traced its tail. A low-tide island appeared.

At six, Eric also turned up, inspecting the erosion of the night. I watched him stooping as he walked, as though into the headwind that had settled with dawn. The stoop was more marked when he was on his own. He came up to say hello, and I asked him if he had backache.

He smiled and said no. 'I've always bent forward a bit.'

'Oh.'

'It's probably because I'm a worrier.'

'We all worry,' I said.

'Yes, but for me it's a way of life. I think it's my retirement plan.'

He said the beach had cut further into the dune. It seemed Eric thought that by living in Sydney I wouldn't notice. 'One day we'll have to move our houses,' I joked.

'With any luck, I'll have followed your father out before that happens.'

'You're not an optimist, then.'

'And you're not as nice as you look,' he quipped.

Others enjoyed the work of the sea, and could relate to the gradual disfigurement. Anthony would find things to draw: a row of trees collapsed down the sand wall; fence posts and railings twisted into rust sculptures. This was where the beach once stopped; this was how far the dune used to come out. 'Don't you think it's a relief to know that it all gets washed away?' he had once said. But I had thought of Eric and my father and the afternoons they spent repairing the path, and replied, 'I think I liked the path where it was.'

31

Eric and Claire understood that there was more to Dad's leaving England, our coming to Australia – a piece of the story that he'd held on to for himself to think about. I'd never known what it was, only that it was there, and that it was quietly expressed in his bearing and in that impenetrable dedication to a wife that he'd lost young. And perhaps that was the part of him that many loved most of all. We knew that one day I would find out, and join his secret to my own story, just as a wave that holds you back when you swim out rushes you to shore when you come back in.

Now, it brought me to Whitby.

As though stepping from the aircraft to the estuary wall, I immediately retraced my infant steps there. At first, my parents and my younger self were almost as strangers – but as the days passed I re-inhabited the town and a sense of us here.

It happened through repetition: for a day I repeated a walk around both sides of the estuary, the little beach, and the streets that bordered the water in uneven steps of red and grey brick houses. I did it until I recovered a sensation held over from childhood, one that brought me their company as I walked, my parents on either side of me.

Also, I had a room near our old house, at a B & B two streets from the water. On the second day, I called Lillie, but the phone rang out. The morning was long and damp: a low, grey sky stuck to the brick-work of the terrace housing until lunchtime, when the atmosphere lifted and retired couples emerged from the other B & Bs, trooping past like the last guard of the British coast. The ruins of Whitby Abbey sat above the town, a perfect witness to the gentle confusion below. A steep line of steps from the waterside rose to a wide field of sodden grass and ponds. From there, the grey-blue edge of the Yorkshire coastline: the Whitby of my parents' life together and, to the south, the open beaches where my mother had drowned.

I found the house, almost felt I knew it. My feet took the streets that led to it, and a narrow set of steps that ran as part easement, part entrance to the door, to where we'd lived until I was four. I knocked on a cloudy glass pane but no one came.

Would I wait for Lillie, or use the day to visit my mother's plot? As strange as it seemed, I'd hoped that Lillie would be home, so that I wouldn't have to go to Mum straight away, for after having rushed to Whitby I felt only shyness towards my mother, the hesita-tion of a long-awaited meeting. But at Lillie's no one came to the door, and seemingly there was nothing else to do but catch the bus to Scarborough, the next town to the south, where my mother had drowned and where her ashes were kept. I caught a bus used mainly by pensioners with shopping carts, and then walked up to the cemetery.

That day, I learnt that my father had left Whitby too soon. Or, sooner than I'd always thought. We'd arrived in Australia a little more than a month after my fourth birthday, on 24 January 1992.

I knew the date precisely: there was the stamp in our passports, and also a ritual he'd instituted after my accident. On that day every year, we took the car for a country drive, inland from Lion's Head, through the dairy-farming land of creek valleys, and villages of half-a-dozen houses, a general store and, if we were lucky, a pub.

Our drive was a way of re-migrating, of insisting we were home – I saw even then that Dad was convincing himself that many of the things he'd left behind could be found in our new country, and I guessed they were things he'd once done with my mother.

So I had no doubt of the date we came to Australia. And yet on my mother's certificate, brought out by a kindly woman at the cemetery who was empowered to release her ashes, the registered date of her death read 14 March 1992. I stared at the date and waited for it to change. To go back to a date before our departure. But it wouldn't.

My father had left before she died, not after.

I heard her voice, and a conversation between the two of them. An argument? At the very least a difference in time: two months that separated what I'd always believed – that we'd left Whitby a year after my mother died – and what I now knew, and barely understood. My father had spent the greater part of his life protecting me from the date of her death.

At last I saw that much in our relationship had grown from there, and that the cost had been a kind of silence between us. Was this the gap that had given him a complex theory of music and me a child's philosophy of swimming out to find her?

But why the lie?

*

213

The next afternoon, through the grey panes of Lillie's front door, I watched the even, wide-hipped approach of Angela, Lillie's part-time nurse. 'Come in out of this,' she said, and took my raincoat. 'You must be Ted.'

She said Lillie was much better. A trip to the hospital yesterday had been exhausting, but she'd had a rest this morning.

'Yes, I came by. No one was home.'

Now, my aunt sat in an armchair. I'd called to say I was coming, but she seemed unready for me to arrive. She held her hand to my face and said she wouldn't get up. I looked at her eyes, which, like her handwriting, took not only the shape but the emphasis of Dad's. But as when she'd visited Lion's Head, it was her hair that you noticed most. The seven years since had aged her, but they hadn't changed that. It was cut short and had thinned into a silver web of curls. As she had then, she clutched at the strands of hair that escaped and fell across her face, as though to remind them to stay still.

Then she concealed the skeletal hands under the top folds of a blanket. I felt that she didn't want me to see them, their cartography of red and blue highways. But they made it out of their confinement and illuminated the things she needed to say: faint gestures, turns of the hand towards an idea or a recollection.

Her health had declined since she last wrote to me; Angie said that it tended to run in cycles. She could well rally again. Lillie muttered that her back was very bad; on the worst days, she even had trouble moving her head and face. She wouldn't be able to speak much today.

I wasn't sure how much she could tell me about my mother's death, but for a week I lingered, and I found myself returning to the house. Her back slowly improved, and each day I wanted to see her once more before I left, if only to say goodbye.

One afternoon I found her suddenly sitting upright watching the soaps. As Angie and I walked into the living room, Lillie switched off the television and said, 'I hoped you might come back. Sit down close. I'm feeling … you know.'

'You're better,' I said. 'You look very well.'

'I am in a state of flux, that's what,' she answered with a breathless laugh. 'I take days like these when they come.'

'Do you mind me being here?'

'I wasn't sure I'd see either of you again. This is so much better. I've had you back for a little.' We turned to face the television, seeing ourselves reflected in the dull screen, seated on either side of an occasional table that was somehow too well preserved. I noticed how far forward I was leaning, as though I was waiting to catch her.

I tried to reassure her: 'What I meant was, I don't want to upset you by coming back and going over old ground.'

She wasn't interested. 'I know what you meant. Do you know what I meant? I meant that I want to talk to you. You think I can give you a little bit of your mother. I can. But what I have from those days is very selfish; it's my treasure. She was *my* friend. First, that's what she was to me. I disagreed with your father, you must know that. He ought to have forgiven her. He ought to have stayed. She deserved that from him. She never stopped loving him. It was his choice to go.'

'I'm sorry – did they separate? Did they get back together?' I didn't quite yet understand what Lillie assumed I knew.

'That's not what I'm talking about.' There was an apology in her eyes. But her expression also said, *Interrupt me less, wait for it.* She went on, 'Your mother and I understood each other very well. She was a friend in a way I hadn't experienced before. I knew her from the inside. I loved her. Everybody said she was beautiful, yes. But I saw where her beauty came from. And your father knew that about her, too. Through and through she was a good person. That's why he should have forgiven her.'

'So ... she left him?' Was that the knowledge that Dad had protected me from: that she had left us?

'Yes.'

'And he wouldn't take her back?'

'He left before she came back. She thought it was too late.'

I turned to Lillie's reflection. 'Are you going to tell me why she left him?'

'Probably not.'

And perhaps I knew enough. Lillie was right; her perspective was different from mine. It seemed she'd waited all these years just to talk about her friendship with Mum. Evidently, that was what she felt she could give me. The rest missed the point.

'Before I met Isabel, Bell, I hadn't known that you could meet yourself, if you understand me. Or that there was such a thing as a complete meeting of souls. I know I never felt it with a man, and I haven't felt it since. I was at home when I was with her.

'We talked about this quite openly, she and I. She felt the same way. It's the reason she left you in my care; I suppose it was also the reason that, in a way, I sided with her against your father. He was wrong and of course he knows it – he knew it.'

'They fought?'

'Yes, they fought and she left. It was a terrible thing for her to do.'

'And then we left, for Australia?'

'Yes. When your father took you away, he asked me to come with you. You and I had grown very close. Bell left when you were three – I took care of you for almost a year. You were starting to see me as your mother. I loved being close to you, but I didn't want that. It wasn't fair on Bell. So I said no. We didn't know where she was, but I told him she'd come back. I stuck by her, Ted, and you must as well. You have to stick by them both. When Isabel died, I only wanted to be alone. I decided that talking about her was impossible, and it's been impossible ever since. I didn't tell anyone that I'd lost my dearest friend. But I've always wanted to tell you.'

She pressed on. 'I came to visit you in Lion's Head to tell you, tell you what a good friend your mother was. I wanted you to know the truth. He wouldn't let me speak about it. He thought it would hurt you too much.'

I felt an urge to turn the television on, flush out the two ghosts around us with a soap opera. I said, 'You did the right thing by staying. You stayed here for her.'

And then I couldn't resist asking. 'What did they fight over?'

'Your father could be possessive. You wouldn't know that.'

'No. It doesn't sound like him at all.'

'He was different with Bell. He wasn't quite himself. He needed her so strongly. And she wasn't to be owned in that way. Isabel was a strong woman.'

'But why leave? Was that a reason to leave us?'

'Yes. But I'm sure she was always coming back.'

I reached for my bag and an envelope. 'I brought a photo with me, of me and my mother, one that my father took when we lived here.' I drew the A4 print out of the bag. 'This is a copy of a picture he gave to me when I was young.'

I handed it to her.

'No,' she said. She held the picture for a moment longer, and then gave it back to me. She was angry about something. 'What did you expect to find here? Did you know that you'd have to deal with all this?'

'I knew there was more.'

'Are you glad you came?'

'Yes, I need to know. It's all come very late, probably too late.'

The television turned itself on. 'Damn thing,' Lillie said. 'Or is it me leaning against the remote?' She searched for the controls in the blanket. 'When did you get that picture?' she asked.

'I was twelve or thirteen. Dad showed it to me, just after the accident.'

'It wasn't taken by your father. It was taken by a friend of Isabel's. I remember the day. Your father went in to get tea, something for us to have by the water, and left them together, with you and me. He took the picture.'

'He?'

'Yes, a friend of Bell's.'

Angie came in with cups, as if to signal that our conversation had come to an end. 'I sleep too much,' Lillie said, seemingly out of nowhere. 'There's nothing you can do about that.'

'You've been asleep mostly when I've come.'

'Yes, I expect so.' She began to stand. 'Wait here.' She didn't want any help. Then she inched towards a letter-writing desk in the hallway, and stopped to examine keys that hung from a band at the back of the desk.

'Let me help you,' I said.

'Yes, actually, give me a hand. It's a damn thing to unlock.'

The lock resisted, and then opened. Lillie stepped in front of me, and from underneath drew out a cloth envelope beaded with buttons. From it, a photograph of my mother.

'What happened between them?' I asked again. 'Did my father leave her because of this other man?'

'No, no.' She shook her head. 'No, she left him. Because your father was so angry.'

'Did she leave us? I mean, did she actually move house?'

'That's right. She left Whitby. She didn't say where she was going. She wrote, but she wouldn't say where she was living. Not even to me. Your father followed a postmark once. He was desperate to find her. She'd sent a letter from London. He went to see if he could find her there. Of course it doesn't mean much to get a letter with a London postmark.'

'Did she write to him again, when she came back?'

'Possibly. She didn't tell me. Have you looked?'

'Yes, but perhaps not well enough.' Only now did it occur to me where he might have kept her letters.

Lillie went on, 'He waited a year. Then he gave up. He said he couldn't wait any longer. He gave me the house and made his plans. That's when he moved to Australia. When the two of you moved.'

'And you didn't agree.'

'I knew she'd come back. But he took it all so badly, because he knew that he'd pushed her away. And he still thought I was just taking Isabel's side. Wouldn't stop saying I should be coming with you. But she was my friend, Ted. I thought that things would come right. Most of all I wanted to be here when she got back. I was here. She came back for you and your father. Yes, I knew she would.'

I walked again along the estuary wall, and returned to my room with the print and its new companion, the photograph that Lillie had given me. I looked at Mum and wondered if she really was happy that day, as I'd long thought. Pictures, as my father hinted, can lie – lit from an invisible point, captured by an invisible hand.

I lay on the bed, and felt again the kindness of his gift that day, after he'd been angry with me for swimming out and had replaced his anger with a photograph. He'd reached for something – if not an apology, then some form of consolation that could only be found in the past, in a lost world. It still existed because it had been captured, perhaps by someone he'd seen as a rival. He showed me a photograph that part of him must have wanted to tear up, but a photograph that he knew I could love.

And now a companion, a colour print of a young woman sitting in the same spot as that day. The estuary wall, rocks painted by rain, the water behind a silver sky of low clouds and sea birds. A last picture of her, taken by Lillie, the one who stayed for her. In her eyes, the invitation, held across the world. *Meet me here.*

Meet me in the water.

32

I walked from the room to the water's edge, and examined the pub signs. I didn't know where I wanted to go. It was a summer Saturday, late afternoon now, and tourists brought a lightness to the river, warmth. The boats drifted by, and were chased by seagulls searching for movement, any sign of food. People caught your eye, and then turned back to their friends. A smile on a sunny day. A surface that shone in the river light.

Walk, I thought. Walk until the tremor is replaced by tiredness, the satisfaction of being merged with the world – dusty, hot, not just into its glare but out of your role as witness, the latecomer.

I needed to be a participant in something. But too soon even the souvenir shops were closing; more dogs were being walked in the last hour of the day; the restaurants bleeding soft light onto the pavements and the awnings.

I sat and drank at a pub for an hour, at a bench on the corner of the esplanade. Then I bought a bottle of scotch from an off-licence and joined a line-up of slightly drunk people at a fish-and-chips shop. Their faces were rosy under the fluorescent bulbs. I took my fish dinner and climbed the steps up to the abbey, found a bench, and watched from under the wide cover of a clear night as the stars came into the world. There was a new one every few minutes.

The food was too greasy. Or I was getting too drunk to care about eating. I couldn't swallow. It was late, but I couldn't stand the thought of going back to my room. I wondered about the length of the bench and whether I'd fit. Fuck it. Nothing bad would happen now, no Whitby mugging. Nothing stranger than going back to a room and my photographs, back to the unreality of a moment when I'd followed my father to his home and found the reason he'd left. No reason to fight it.

I missed him. I wanted only to be back in Lion's Head, near his ashes. I wanted to speak to Claire, tell her that in the end I'd done as he'd asked. I'd left the ashes in his study, and come for my mother on my own.

I'm drowning, I thought. *If I stay under for a moment longer I'll stop breathing*. Had I learnt that yet? That it can happen. But there was no release in drowning. There couldn't be. I cried, as though there were release in that. Stupid tears as I leant against the bench. I collapsed, not wanting to stop myself, the lunatic sobbing on his own in the park, and there was something very calm in it.

I looked again along the bench. Too short. But I rolled down and hung my legs over the end. A constellation of ocean lights still brighter below, all part of the reflections of pubs and shopfronts and stars. Too drunk. From the bench I rolled onto the grass, fell. I covered my face. It was ridiculous, I saw it. I stopped crying at last, and laughed. And then I fell asleep.

I woke at first light. The scotch was gone; I thought someone had finished it for me. I checked my wallet and my watch. It was five.

'My mother died after we left,' I said out loud, hoping there might be a way for her to hear me from Lion's Head. 'She died of a swimming accident after we left.'

Then you were right. She was with you all along; she was swimming with you.

'What are you doing?' I asked.

I thought you wanted me.

'And you came.'

I sat up. 'Why did you leave for the farm? Have you ever tried to work it out?'

I can't work it out on my own. Is that what she would say?

Or, *Come back.*

There is always a way back. It lies in the future, I know, but much of it also lies in the past. In a hangover in Whitby, and in that summer before Anthony and Claire moved to Sydney, in how our souls had selected each other.

I returned from Whitby. I came straight into the study and finally took out my father's old recording of *I Puritani*, and there found the last letter from Mum to him. In it, she said that she was back in Whitby and that Lillie had told her we'd left only shortly before. Could she come to Lion's Head, join us here and try to start again? He'd written a letter in reply, but kept it here with hers, unsent. I wondered if he hoped that one day I'd find them. In the end, there had been no reason to send it, but then no reason to keep it, either. It had been intercepted by the news that Mum had died.

He'd written, *Yes, come over.* We'd be waiting for her here – in the end, in a letter hidden in a record sleeve, like a spot of light inside the circle of smoke. But also they were together at last, for

I'd brought my mother's ashes back to Lion's Head, and now I put them beside his.

I like them here with me. In love, as they loved each other. Across the dull ache of a foreign line: the waterline, the scar on the stomach. *Try not to fuss with it*, I still hear him say.

Claire comes in and asks, 'Have you been up all night?'

'Yes, writing.'

She looks outside. 'I think I'll go for a swim,' she says.

Through the pines, the sun flickers an opening. Seems to promise, as soon as you get in, you'll be back again and the world can start.

But first Claire asks, instead, 'Do you want to come to bed?'

She fetches a glass of water and follows me into the bedroom. On this side of the house, the pines that once stood over my room, deciding what light would make it, have only grown higher and thicker, and now block the morning sun more completely. I feel Claire's hand against the small of my back, touching me.

'Turn around,' she says. Her hand finds mine. She kisses me and pushes me onto the bed. We seem to fall asleep straight away. And then, 'Are you awake?'

'Yes.'

'You were asleep.'

'No.'

'Yes, you were.'

I'm facing away. She puts her arm around me. 'Do you want to talk?'

'No.'

'I love you?' she asks. 'Are you going to say that?'

'I love you.'

'You want me to tell you something?'

'Yes.'

'Go for a swim.'

'When will you start painting again?' I ask in return.

Claire takes her hand away, rolls onto her back. 'When I've got time.'

I start to laugh, but I want her to think about it. 'We could set up a studio.'

'I don't need a studio. My paintings aren't big enough for a studio.'

'But a separate area.'

Small branches break onto the roof. 'How did you ever sleep? It's such a noisy house.'

'I didn't want to. I used to get angry with myself in the mornings when I woke up and realised that I'd fallen asleep. I'd lie here trying not to drop off, and the next thing I knew it was morning and Dad was in the kitchen making coffee. Humming. That was the first thing I heard, him humming. I never noticed that the house was noisy. And then I'd decide that the next night I was going to stay up after him, and beat him to the kitchen in the morning.'

'Did you manage it?'

'No.'

'You stayed up last night.'

She rolls back to face me, and I feel her breath, and a reminder of wine on it. 'Let's go down to the beach,' she suggests, as she sits up. I reach for her waist. But she resists, and puts on a singlet. 'Put your shorts on,' she says, and stands up and walks towards the window.

'Is it open?' I ask.

'Yes.'

'The trees were much lower. You'd get the moon. Even at night I could see across the road.'

I join her by the window. There's blue morning light over the yard. I put one leg out of the window, and feel for the folded metal over the wooden stump. Then I jump down backwards onto wet grass.

'I'm out!' I whisper, although there's no reason to be quiet. 'Come down.'

We cross the yard and then the dirt road, and stop for a moment on the other side. Then Claire runs up the beach path, laughing. 'You can sit and watch if you want,' she tells me.

She glances back over her shoulder, and the sun does its contracted work, and convinces me that, in all things, time is nothing, only ever a beginning. She is fourteen again, a year older than me and as impossible still, too beautiful, as perhaps she's meant to be.

'Are you going to swim?' she asks.

There's only the slightest wave, less than a breath. But it's the sea's invitation, given as openly as before.

Acknowledgments

I would like to express my sincere thanks to the University of Queensland Press. In particular, I am indebted to Madonna Duffy, Judith Lukin-Amundsen and Ian See for their support and careful editing of the manuscript. Their feedback and suggestions have greatly improved this novel, and I'm very grateful for their help and enthusiasm.

Also by Kári Gíslason
THE PROMISE OF ICELAND

In 1990, at the age of seventeen, Kári Gíslason travelled to Iceland, the land of his birth, and arranged to meet his father. What he found was not what he expected.

Born from a secret liaison between his British mother and Icelandic father, Kári moved regularly between Iceland, England and Australia. He grew up aware of who his father was, but understood his mother had promised never to reveal his father's identity. It was a promise his father would also ask him to keep.

A decade later, Kári made the decision to break that promise, and he contacted his half-siblings, who knew nothing of his existence. What led him to this decision and what followed makes for a heartfelt and riveting journey traversing landscapes, time and memory, of one man's search for a sense of belonging.

'Gorgeously told ... a quietly moving and affecting memoir ... Highly recommended.'

Krissy Kneen, *Avid Reader*

'[A] memorable, finely crafted book.'

The Age

'A deeply charming account of displacement, of not really knowing where you come from and how that makes it difficult to know where you belong.'

The Sunday Mail

'A powerful memoir about landscape and identity.'

The Advertiser

ISBN 978 0 7022 3906 9